PENGUIN BOOKS

1755

CLOSED CIRCUIT

WILLIAM HAGGARD

O. 25

CLOSED CIRCUIT

WILLIAM HAGGARD

PENGUIN BOOKS

Penguin Books Ltd, Harmondsworth, Middlesex
U.S.A.: Penguin Books Inc., 3300 Clipper Mill Road, Baltimore 11, Md
AUSTRALIA: Penguin Books Pty Ltd, 762 Whitehorse Road,
Mitcham, Victoria

—

First published by Cassel 1960
Published by Penguin Books 1962
Reprinted 1963

—

Copyright © William Haggard, 1960

—

Made and printed in Great Britain
by C. Nicholls & Company Ltd
Set in Monotype Times

CHAPTER ONE

IN his room in the Foreign Office Kenneth Gibb was waiting for Francis Mason. He was smiling a smile which people who didn't like him – and they were more than he suspected – would have said was superior. He himself would have chosen 'detached' or 'impersonal', for he was far too intelligent to court avoidable dislike. To be disliked was a liability professionally and Kenneth Gibb was essentially a professional. He sat in his room waiting for Francis Mason. Francis Mason was in trouble.

In Kenneth Gibb's considered, his consciously balanced opinion, the trouble was inevitable. Unconsciously his instinct was also that it was deserved, though this he would never have said. But one couldn't live for ever as the Masons did, not even in Candoro. Politics changed – other countries' and Her Majesty's Government's; events marched on. Professionally it wasn't necessary to ask where: what was necessary was to recognize the stream, to flow with it.

Which Francis Mason, or to be scrupulous his absurd old grandfather, didn't seem able to do. As a consequence the heat was on them – the heat of the Candoran summer and of a changing social scene.

Gibb's smile became a little less chill, for now he was genuinely amused. He was remembering what the greenest of recruits to his Service, a colleague scarcely less inexperienced, had told him. The colleague's first post had, just before the war, been somewhere in Eastern Europe, and it was his opinion that if anybody had it coming to them it was the East European landowners. The excellent young man had still been pop-eyed. He had been asked to the country for what he had carefully learnt to call a Friday-to-Monday, to some castle or other, some family with an ancient but unpronounceable name. And it had shaken him. There had been a couple of private aeroplanes on the enormous frozen lawn, Rolls-Royces by the bagful. They had dined in state, a servant behind each chair. Their liveries had been magnificent, their feet, in the bitter winter, shoeless. The plate had been gold, the broken windows stuffed with newspaper. And, my dear, the bathroom! There had apparently been only one, a sort of concrete dam across the corner of what had been a lumber-room. In the rest of the room had been a coke-fired boiler. No window. Milady had gone there when the whimsy took her, dropping her furs on the floor. When the water cooled she rang a handbell. A manservant appeared; bowed politely; stoked the boiler. A man, my dear! But of course he didn't count. He was a servant, less than human.

Yes, they had had it coming to them.

Not, Gibb reflected, that the English in Candoro, the *estancia*-owners, had ever behaved like that. For one thing they were far too sensible, for another too inescapably of their race. But in their way they had been just as obtuse for, generation on generation's heels, they had made the same assumption, unspoken but fatal. ... This will last my time.

And now it hadn't, now the Masons were in trouble. Francis Mason had been sent, understandably if you knew him, by that queer old Clegg – sent from Candoro to consult Kenneth Gibb. Gibb knew Candoro, for he had served there. There was Her Majesty's ambassador at the capital of course, but ...

Kenneth Gibb allowed himself a shrug. He wasn't precisely conceited, but he was aware that the best sort of ambassador, the up-and-coming one, wasn't posted to Candoro. It was the final posting for a respectable failure, whereas Kenneth Gibb ...

Kenneth Gibb could go to the top, Kenneth Gibb meant to.

He smiled his thinnish smile again. Francis Mason was an excellent type, a thoroughly decent fellow. It was a pity he hadn't any brains.

Francis Mason turned left from Downing Street under the archway, right again and up the stairs into the lobby of the Foreign Office. He stated his business, and a receptionist, a trifle off-handedly, helped him fill in a form. He was a little early for his appointment and, his form completed, he sat down quietly to wait. He was glad of the opportunity to collect himself, for he had come from Candoro, from Seven, to ask a favour. That wasn't something which embarrassed him: generous-spirited, he could ask a favour of a friend as easily as he could do one. Of a friend, though – that was important. He wasn't at all sure that Kenneth Gibb was a friend. He admired him, admired his brains.

It was a pity you couldn't trust him farther than you could throw him.

6

Francis Mason put the thought behind him, a little ashamed of what he would have admitted was an instinct. He was a man who, living much with animals, with people known since childhood, trusted his instincts in default of the worldly experience which he knew he lacked. Just the same, it was stupid to come to Kenneth Gibb mistrusting him. For one thing, that sort of feeling couldn't be hidden. In man as in beast it exuded; it almost smelt. Kenneth Gibb would pick it up. By instinct. Or if he hadn't instincts he would use what served him in their stead: his intelligence, his really excellent intelligence.

Francis Mason unaffectedly admired it, or he wouldn't have agreed to Granclegg's proposal that he should fly to England to see him. In the height of summer, too. Summer was always difficult with cattle.

He looked about him in the lobby, faded, a little too casually impressive. Frock-coated messengers were amiably present, and behind the barrier the girl who had received him was talking to another caller in an accent which she did not use at home. A telephone rang on her desk and she answered it.

'Mr Gibb will see you, sir.'

'Thank you,' Francis said politely. Courtesy was another of his instincts. In Candoro it paid; it was indeed a necessity in intercourse with a people proud, mixed, emerging from what in effect had been subservience. It was something which, if not inherent, was a lesson to be learned. But old Clegg Mason seemed never to have done so. If he had, his grandson thought grimly, he mightn't be here in London, coming to see Kenneth Gibb, asking his help to save Seven.

Francis Mason followed a messenger across the lobby with his slightly unsteady horseman's gait. They got into the lift, climbing three floors. A second messenger took Francis from the first. There was another waiting-room. Presently the other messenger returned. 'Mr Gibb will see you, sir.'

It seemed to be a formula.

'Thank you,' Francis said again.

Kenneth Gibb rose to meet him, smiling one of his several smiles, the welcoming one. 'It's good to see you again,' he said easily.

'It's kind of you to spare the time.'

Francis Mason sat down, looking levelly at Kenneth Gibb. He

7

was thinking that his appearance hadn't changed much since he had stayed at Seven. He was very much the diplomatist, the youngish diplomat going places. He had lost a little more hair, but he didn't play the fool with what was left – no growing it long at the sides, no slicking it across his scalp. What hair he had he still wore short, for his well-shaped head could carry a moderate baldness. He was dressed not too carefully, and his features were firm. In later life his eyebrows would be formidable. Francis Mason knew that he was thirty-nine.

Kenneth Gibb in turn inspected Mason. Francis had very long legs, and he sat in a chair a fraction too low for them. He gave the impression that he was riding a little shorter than was comfortable. His clothes were good, London-made, but it was evident that he didn't wear them often. Presently he said, 'Grandfather asked to be remembered to you.'

The sentence was simple, but Francis had considered it. Clegg Mason was Granclegg to his family and Old Clegg to everybody else who spoke English within seventy miles. That, in Candoro, wasn't a particularly long way. But Francis would call him Grandfather until somebody else called him otherwise.

Which Kenneth Gibb did at once. 'Granclegg?' he asked. 'That was nice of him. How is he?'

Privately Francis considered this a slight presumption, but his bright blue eyes, wide-set, did not flicker. 'Very well. Fighting fit still.'

Gibb laughed. 'Fighting ...?' he said, spreading his hands, smiling, this time, his conspirator's, his understanding smile.

'He's a fighter, you know.'

'I do know. That's the trouble. It's very bad luck. On you, I mean. Very bad luck indeed.'

Kenneth Gibb fell into silence, waiting for Francis to go on. It was his personal opinion that it wasn't bad luck at all: it was nemesis deserved. He knew the story. Old Clegg had ridden Romero off his land, off Seven. Romero, then, had been some third-rate local *político* and his demands had become unreasonable. There were a dozen ways old Clegg could have dealt with him, but he had chosen the worst. But it must have been something to have seen, Gibb reflected, as certainly it had become a legend. Old Clegg, rising seventy even then; Miguel, that servant of his; a peon. . . . They had been much better mounted, and they had ridden him like a steer, the two Candorans on the wings, Clegg Mason behind, his legs quite straight in silver stirrups, sitting bolt upright in a Mexican saddle. They had ridden with purpose, not pressing him, silently. Twenty minutes, twenty-five perhaps, to the boundary fence. They had slowed to let him open the gate and, beyond it, he had stopped, staring back in hate. He had started to trot away.

... That trot. If he had galloped, perhaps, even cantered. But to trot, cool, insolent still. ...

Old Clegg couldn't take it. He had got him with the bolas.

The bolas – *las boleadores*! Why, they were almost ready for the museum. Some of the older peons could still use them, and at fairs, in play at country junketings, still did. But never at their work. Cattle today, valuable Herefords, weren't something to risk breaking a leg. But old Clegg Mason still carried them. They were his hobby. Both sorts – the tripper, the hobbler, and the other, the one-ball killer. On Romero he had used the less lethal, but with a trotting horse the result had been inevitable. Romero hadn't landed *parado* – he had been fortunate not to break something. He had caught his horse again, for it had been tired and never a good one, and he had ridden away.

He had ridden away to become, six years later, President of Candoro.

... And what would you make of that? But Kenneth Gibb hadn't in fact a doubt. You would make of it that Clegg's grandson was now in London asking your help. God knew he needed it.

But he was still urbane, wholly impersonal, as he repeated :
'Very bad luck indeed.'

'Who would have thought that tin-pot grafter ...?'

'Would be President of Candoro.'

'Dictator,' Francis said.

Kenneth Gibb's expression sharpened almost imperceptibly. 'He's a Head of State,' he said. His manner was austere.

'What's the difference?'

'Well ... I suppose it's a bit constitutional. Sometimes dictators manoeuvre behind puppet presidents; sometimes they go the whole hog and openly take power.'

'I know,' Francis Mason's mind worked simply but perfectly lucidly. This was a distinction without a difference.

Kenneth Gibb changed tack at once. 'The real difference,' he went on, 'is in method rather than in form. European dictator-ships, for instance, ask all of you. In Europe, if you don't think rightly, the secret police calls in the small hours. But in South America' – he shrugged, excusing the generalization – 'in South America my impression was that provided you kept your mouth shut, minded your own business, and paid your taxes, nothing very dreadful happened to you.'

'I dare say you're right. ... And provided you don't make personal enemies.'

'Quite so.'

'As we have.'

'I'm afraid so.'

'You were talking about taxes. Taxes are in point.'

'Yes?'

'We have a bridge, you know – we built it ourselves. The river cuts Seven in half: it would put us out of business not to have a bridge. We let anybody use it, and we never charge. Equally we never seem to have got permission to build across what we don't own.'

'So?'

'So we've got to pull it down and wait for Romero to build an-other. Not much of a chance, I should say, and if he did the tolls would be ruinous. Alternatively we can keep the bridge and pay a tax for it.'

'How much?'

'Five thousand a year.'

Gibb whistled softly, but he was thinking too. 'Nobody else has a bridge? I don't remember one, but I wasn't a visitor at Seven for long enough to be certain. For instance, not the Ken-dricks at six?'

'Nobody else has land on both sides.'

Kenneth Gibb was silent again. Finally, he said slowly, depre-catingly: 'He's after you all right.'

'I know it. And that isn't all. There's our title to the land.'

'But surely that's in order?'

'We always assumed it after four generations. But a lawyer called the other day, a man from the capital. Very polite, he was. So Granclegg dug the document out from some other lawyer. We've a perpetual lease.'

'Which turns out not to exist in Candoran law?'

10

'So our lawyer warned us.'

'But what about the other *estancias?*'

'They were bought for value – freehold or its equivalent.'

Kenneth Gibb stared at the wall for some time before he said: 'It'll be money, I imagine.'

'I suppose so.'

'It's a good thing you've plenty.'

'Yes ... in a way. We make a good living, but you can't sell pieces of a working *estancia*, or strip it of stock. You can't sell your tools and live.'

'Have you anything outside Candoro?'

'A bit. Granclegg got it over here a few years ago. I never knew how.'

'It might work,' Gibb said. He was thinking that they were all the same, these Anglo-Candorans. They could never see farther than their noses; they never noticed change, considered the future. Well, perhaps Francis Mason didn't need to. He and Lavinia were childless. There had been a daughter once, but she had died as a baby. They never mentioned her. 'I'll help you if I can,' he said.

'It's very good of you.'

'We're not without weapons. Your grandfather can't go to Romero directly – that's obvious – but his brother is their ambassador here. That could help.'

'That's why I'm here. They say he's a sensible fellow; they say he's approachable.'

'Dickie Romero is certainly approachable.'

Francis Mason hid a smile ... Dickie Romero! His name wasn't Dickie or anything like it. But it must be the thing to call an ambassador Dickie. He wasn't quite sure what thing, and he wasn't quite sure that the familiarity didn't jar. But his expression hadn't changed as he asked: 'You could put me in touch?'

'Of course I could. Actually I'll do better; I'll give you a line to Menderez. He's first secretary, but in practice he runs the show. In any case it'd probably be a mistake to go to the top too quickly.' Kenneth Gibb smiled his professional smile again. 'The important thing is to put the penny into the right slot to start with. Then it may drop.'

'It's very good of you,' Francis repeated.

Kenneth Gibb did not answer; instead he began to write on his

11

best writing-paper. He wrote slowly, in a fine italic hand which he had just acquired. He put his letter in an envelope and sealed it. Then he picked up his telephone, speaking briefly. 'Menderez is in,' he said finally. 'He'll see you now. You'll find somebody you know there, by the way.'

'Oh?'

'Clare Kendrick.'

'Oh,' Francis said again. But his tone had changed.

Gibb didn't seem to notice it; he gave Francis Mason his letter of introduction.

'I'd better go at once.'

'It might be wise.'

'And thank you again.'

'Not at all. Lunch with me tomorrow and tell me how it went.'

'I'd like to.'

'Until tomorrow, then.'

Francis found a taxi setting down in the courtyard, and in his room Kenneth Gibb looked at his watch. It was half past five. That idiot Mason would be at least an hour at the Candorans'.

An hour with Lavinia. . . .

They would have to be discreet, of course. But after all he had stayed at Seven.

It could be just a social call.

CHAPTER TWO

CANDORO, a secession state, had split from its much larger neighbour to the south a few years after the latter itself had broken from Spanish rule. Its history had been odd in the extreme. In the early nineteenth century and whilst it was still Spanish the English, for no very evident reason, had landed a ship's complement of Marines and had burnt to the ground what was then the capital of a province. They had been notably more successful than their Scottish brothers-in-arms whose colours, still disgraced, hang in the church of Santo Domingo considerably to the south. But a few years later Canning, again for no obvious reason, lent to the now independent state what at the time was a large sum of money. For no obvious reason, but it had been a remarkable investment. The British poured into Candoro: it became in effect a colony, though never in name, since its technical independence flattered a man called James Monroe.

The British hadn't objected, for the trappings of political authority didn't particularly attract them. They held the reality of economic power: emigrants of British stock in practice ran Candoro as in fact they owned most of it.

Amongst the emigrants had been the Masons, the first of them in the eighteen-thirties, a clockmaker. He had prospered and had bought land. His son in turn had prospered and, by the time the huge tracts north of the river were ripe for development, this Mason had possessed the capital to accept one. Accept had been the word, for the Candoran state, still struggling between neighbours who would gladly have engulfed it, hadn't been particular. If a man had resources to work a large new estate he was more than welcome to it; indeed he was a benefactor.

Seven of these *estancias* had been carved out along the tributary where the Mason land now lay, others elsewhere. The Mason's was the Seventh, and it was still called the Seven. This wasn't arrogance since, though the estate had another and floridly Spanish name, the native Candoran never used it. He spoke a Spanish which a Spaniard, or at any rate a Castilian, would have understood with difficulty; he couldn't be bothered with Estancia of the

13

Flowering Chestnut. In any case there wasn't a flowering chestnut.

On Seven, then, Clegg Mason and Francis still sat, living in circumstances, an aura, roughly comparable to the Argentina of the nineteen-thirties. They were the last of these Anglo-Candoran families to trace their descent to the original grant-holder, and old Clegg at least was a little suspicious of those who had replaced them. Not all these newcomers were British by blood, for life in Candoro had changed and was changing. But whatever their race they were men who had bought their estates as going concerns; men who had taken in the process a new and better title to them. They hadn't, as had the Masons, built their first house with their own hands, building again later in a solid modesty. On the contrary some of them had replaced what they had found – perhaps the second or third house on the site – with Scottish baronial castles or houses from Sunningdale golf course, importations, Clegg Mason considered, and suspect of a certain decadence. For the not-so-distant *estancia*-owner in Argentina old Clegg had a tolerant contempt. Why, he knew a man in Argentina, a cripple, who ran his ranch from a jeep. Clegg Mason admired his courage. . . .

. . . But a jeep!

At least Charles Kendrick still rode: as a neighbour at Six he wasn't impossible. He was in fact a very shrewd man, having slipped out of Argentina in 1946. He and Clegg Mason were on the most amicable terms, but Kendrick had never told him how he got his money out. Clegg Mason thought him a trifle effete, his English airs a little too exaggerated; but he admired his business sense. He approved even when, against all precedent, he and his wife had adopted a Candoran girl. There had been some mystery about her birth. Not that that mattered. Old Clegg had grown extremely fond of her.

They had named her Clare, Clare Kendrick, and at this moment she sat in the Candoran embassy waiting for Francis Mason. She was what the embassy was pleased to call a confidential secretary, which meant that she was something a little superior to the London-recruited girls who did the ordinary typing, but not so superior that she couldn't be asked to make tea. She had been pleased and surprised to get the job, for the Anglo-Candoran, though indubitably a Candoran national, wasn't as things were a popular candidate for the Candoran Foreign Service. Still, Charles Kendrick had been influential, and, Clare remembered, she hadn't in fact a drop of English blood. Not a drop.

It didn't worry her as she painted her lips, for her image in the mirror was reassuring. Her dark hair, fashionably short, clung to her head in a firm bell; her olive skin was immaculate. Her mouth was wide, a promise of generosity. In repose her face held a hint of immobility, a hint of a blood other than Spanish, but in laughter, in any emotion, it could flare in a sudden vitality. She wasn't tall but she was beautifully made. She moved superbly.

She looked in the mirror again, not worried that she wasn't English. But she was very worried. It hadn't been difficult to discover why Francis was in England.

Francis Mason might be ground exceeding small.

She had already arranged that he be shown to her room, and the porter brought him in.

'Hullo, Francis.'

'Hullo, Clare.' He took her hand, holding it for an instant. She could guess what he was thinking and it didn't displease her.

'I'm afraid I've bad news for you.'

'You'd better shoot it then.'

'Menderez rang down ten minutes ago. I couldn't catch you at the Foreign Office to stop you. He's afraid he can't see you after all.'

'I see,' Francis said. He lit a cigarette before he added: 'So I'm getting the treatment.'

She liked the way he said it. His candid face was disappointed, but he spoke without resentment, wholly without self-pity. He stood before her in his unaccustomed London clothes, tall, a little straighter than usual under what was clearly a blow. He had achieved a very creditable smile.

'You mustn't jump to conclusions. He said it was important and it might be. At any rate he's left the office. And he said he'd ring you; he told me to take your number.'

'We're staying at Parker's.'

Clare Kendrick wrote it down. 'I'll ring you.'

'I hope so, I'll have to ring back if you don't.'

They stood for a moment almost awkwardly. 'I'll help you if I can,' Clare said suddenly.

15

'God knows I need it.' He took her hand again; held it another moment; was gone.

Clare Kendrick sat down quickly, wanting him fiercely, telling herself she did not.

Francis Mason began to walk from Belgrave Square to Parker's. It wasn't the most fashionable hotel in London, and if your taste ran to cocktail bars, to chrome and slick lifts, it was actively tatty. But if you liked solid comfort, service so perfect you never noticed it, Parker's was ideal. It was always full, and often with Americans. Mostly they came from Boston.

Francis, frowning, swung his umbrella. He was thinking that it would have been pleasant to have taken Clare to dinner. There were excellent reasons why he should not – excellent, overwhelming principles which he accepted. But it wasn't so easy to accept the immediate reason. It irritated him. He had another engagement ... and he hadn't. Lavinia had said something about a theatre, something well short of a definite date. But if she did want to go and he wasn't available she would consider he had let her down. And say so. And if she stayed at home, had one of those heads of hers, real or imagined, it wouldn't occur to her that she had bespoken an evening and defaulted. A rare evening in London.

He walked into Parker's, asking the porter for his wife. 'She's in the drawing-room, sir.' At Parker's 'lounge' was unthinkable.

Kenneth Gibb rose easily as he came in. 'You've been pretty quick at the Candorans',' he said.

Francis Mason admired his aplomb. No excusing himself, no talk about paying a call on a hostess from Candoro: instead half a glance at the flowers on the table, still in their paper. It was all very expert, beautifully correct. And more than a little absurd. He *had* had hospitality at Seven. Three times – no, four. And that was a little odd. The capital was admittedly dull, as stuffily bourgeois as Zürich: young men imprisoned there were often glad of a few days' air at Seven. Young men who rode or shot. But Kenneth Gibb did neither. He had sat in the comfortable ranchhouse chatting to Lavinia.

She had seemed to enjoy it. Enormously.

'You were pretty quick at the Candorans',' Gibb repeated.

'Menderez wouldn't see me.'

16

Kenneth Gibb's expression changed immediately. 'That was rather rude,' he said precisely.

'To me?'

'To both of us.'

'He said he'd telephone. Clare Kendrick told me.'

'I'll remind him if he doesn't.' Kenneth Gibb was genuinely annoyed. He was friendly enough with Menderez; he might even have liked him if he didn't say such shattering, such grossly unprofessional things. The habit was exceedingly disturbing – not one to risk intimacy with. In any case one couldn't overlook the matter of rank. He, Kenneth Gibb, was Grade Six – a Counsellor. Menderez was First Secretary. To jump an appointment formally requested . . .

It had been a discourtesy.

'Clare Kendrick,' Lavinia Mason said. She was looking at her husband.

'Yes. She's working at the embassy.'

'I knew that, Francis.'

There was a moment of silence.

'I gather she likes it.'

'I'm glad. . . . Did she send any message?'

'Well. . . . We were talking business, you know. It was all very hurried.' Francis Mason was a very poor liar.

'I see,' Lavinia said.

Kenneth Gibb rose smoothly. 'I must be going.'

'So soon?'

'I'm afraid so,' For a moment Gibb hesitated. 'I suppose we couldn't meet later this evening. All three of us. A theatre perhaps.'

'I'm sorry, I'm simply not up to it.' Lavinia Mason looked at her husband coolly. 'We're spending the evening in,' she said.

Clare Kendrick locked up her office, and at six walked to her tiny flat. She began to make tea. The Kendricks were great tea-drinkers and she had caught the habit. She made her tea carefully, warming the pot, being generous with the tea itself, letting the brew stand a little under a cosy. Then she poured it, sniffing luxuriously. She didn't smoke, and her senses were acute. The smell of fresh tea was at least as delicious as its taste. People didn't seem to realize that, or perhaps they couldn't. You saw them swigging it, swilling it down. ... Not that most tea was drinkable.

She curled on her bed, kicking off her shoes. She would have admitted that she was miserable. It was easy to hate a woman whose man you wanted, tempting to seek allies in your dislike of her. Just the same they existed. Not other women, either: women would comfort you publicly, despise you in private. Not women then, but men. Sensible, reliable men – her father and old Clegg Mason. She could remember it perfectly.

It had been three years ago. She had been sixteen then – a woman in Candoro – and napping on a sofa in the sitting-room. Her father and Clegg Mason had come in suddenly. Old Clegg had been angry, evidently continuing a subject already defined. 'It's a tragedy,' he was saying.

'Lavinia's your problem, of course, not mine. But I'll admit I've never taken to her.'

Whisky gurgled from a decanter; soda splashed. Clare Kendrick peeped out from the sofa. She was fond of her father, but beside Clegg Mason he struck her as faintly absurd. Old Clegg was lean and grey and angry, and anger suited him. Charles Kendrick was what she had heard called a fine figure of a man. He was in fact a little overweight – not grossly, Clare thought: about a stone – and now he was puffing, pulling his handsome moustache. His clothes were a thought too consciously English. 'I'd wondered if he and Clare ...' he said slowly.

'I wish to God he'd taken her.'

Clare Kendrick on her sofa made herself very small. She was committed now. Sixteen – a woman! And eavesdropping. ...

It was shameful, shameless. Her cheeks began to burn.

She did not move.

'It'd have been a damned good thing.' Charles Kendrick was fond of 'damned', thought 'bloody' a little too much. Clegg Mason swore as he fancied. 'Six and Seven joined,' Kendrick went on. 'Quite a holding, eh?'

'I hadn't considered that.' Old Clegg was a trifle cool. 'What I wanted was a decent wife for Francis.'

'What the devil did he see in Lavinia?'

'What wasn't there. It was a sort of rebound – reaction, rather.'

'I didn't know there was another girl.'

Clegg Mason clucked irritably. 'There wasn't. It wasn't as simple as that.'

'Then I don't know what you mean.'

Clare Kendrick couldn't see him, but old Clegg seemed to be collecting his thoughts. 'Have you ever been in Francis's room?' he asked suddenly.

'Never.'

'It would surprise you. Books, gramophone records, a picture or two. He's a very good cattleman but he isn't a roughneck. You never met his mother, did you? He knows his job, but that isn't all of him. Not like me. I'm a has-been, uneducated –'

'I wouldn't say –' Charles Kendrick began ponderously.

'Save your breath – I wasn't fishing. The point is Francis, and he isn't wholly beef-breeder. He'll run this place when I die – I think it's time I did. But he wants more than that.'

'Which in England he went looking for? Which he thought Lavinia had?'

'Exactly. And she hasn't.'

Clare Kendrick heard glasses refilling; presently her father said: 'Of course I never met the Smarts.'

'I did; I flew over for the wedding.'

'What were they like?'

'Bogus. Father Smart was a doctor in a country town. There were four of them in the practice, and I suppose he was making a thousand a year pre-war. But they didn't live like that; they were what I should call near-County. Mrs Smart had the money – linen, I think it was; Mrs Smart had the say-so. She wasn't a bad wife, but Smart was a cipher in the house. They made him retire.'

'Not very healthy for the children.'

'Of course it wasn't. Country G.P.s are excellent stock, but they don't cross kindly with off-beat gentry.'

'I raise cattle myself,' Kendrick said.

'Then we're talking the same language. The household was a total sham. I don't blame Francis – he hadn't been to England since his school days. Seven is comfortable, I suppose, but it isn't exactly civilized. So he goes to England, half of him starved, and he gets taken in.'

'I'm beginning to understand.'

'It was all there on the surface, though – the pretty manners, the superficial knowledge. Gauguin and the latest novel. In fact they didn't know a thing: hard knowledge, hard-won, Mrs Smart would have despised. I think she would have thought it rather common.'

'She sounds a bitch.'

'Not a bitch: there were dozens like her. Just blood not to breed with.'

'But why did Lavinia take him? It must have been something, you know – leaving that sort of life for Seven.'

'She was getting on; she's a year or two older than Francis. You can guess her life – jobs in London for a month or two, playing at them; getting the sack; creeping home. Plenty of money always, parties . . .'

'Pretty futile,' Kendrick said.

'A dead blind alley. And she was getting a bit of a name, too. I found that out afterwards. "Those Smart girls" . . .'

'As bad as that?'

'One mustn't exaggerate – I expect it was nothing. Anyway, she went quite to pieces here.'

Inevitably, Clare thought.

There was a pause. 'Not one to breed from,' Kendrick said.

'They haven't done much breeding, have they?' Clegg exploded suddenly. 'One bloody baby – a girl. And dead. What the devil's the use of that?'

'Didn't the doctor say she couldn't have another?'

'So she tells us.'

'Meaning?'

'Meaning what I say. I could hardly ask him even if I cared. I know they sleep separately.'

'It's a mess.'

There was a long, masculine silence before Clegg Mason said: 'We were talking about cattle, about blood . . . Also about Clare.'

'You know who her father was?'

'I think so.'

'And her mother?'

'I can guess. There are quite a few of them about still. In Candoro, that is. We never quite killed them off. Not like those bloody *Argentinos*. Good stock, too. Tough, hardy. . . .'

'Excellent wives.'

'And in Clare's case charming.'

'You wouldn't have objected, then?'

20

'Man, I'd have jumped at it. Oh well ... May I see the new silo?'

Clare Kendrick had climbed off the sofa. She was very angry indeed. ... Discussing her as though she were a cow, Francis that new Hereford bull. Four figures he had cost, and more – a fortune. But goodness, he could do his job. She smiled, but anger was unabated. What a way to talk! It had been lucid and logical and male; only one thing was wrong with it: they hadn't, not for a moment, considered Clare Kendrick. She might not want him, she might have other ideas.

It was something to enrage a saint. It was infuriating – she might not love him.

It was intolerable when she did.

CHAPTER THREE

FRANCIS MASON, though with difficulty, had waited next day till noon; then he telephoned to Clare.

'There's nothing,' she said unhappily. 'Menderez hasn't been in this morning. I don't know where he is.'

'But he left no message?'

'I'm afraid not.'

Clare Kendrick broke the silence which followed. 'I'll help you, Francis,' she said again. 'If I can. I *mean* to.'

'Clare ...' Finally but not hopefully Francis said: 'I'm lunching with Kenneth Gibb. Perhaps he'll know what's happening.' He rang off abruptly.

Clare put the receiver down, her straight black eyebrows frowning in thought. Her tiny office overlooked the embassy's formal garden, and it was very quiet. Clare too was quiet, thinking a little wryly that decency had its drawbacks: Francis Mason was at a disadvantage. A cad would have been at home in this, bluffing, threatening back, quite possibly succeeding. Or one of your subtle men, wholly without principle ... Principle – sticking, for instance, to a wife you must detest. Decency was at a disadvantage, and today at something of a discount. All right, let them discount it. They could have their gutter *bravos*.

Francis wasn't easily excited: living with Granclegg no sensible man would be. A sensible man at Seven would be unassertive, agreeing whenever it was possible, giving the answers which would please. He might even seem a little over-tolerant. Clare Kendrick was certain Francis wasn't over-tolerant. Pushed beyond habitual courtesy, seriously wronged, Francis Mason would be suddenly Clegg's grandson.

But that was something to be avoided – certainly it was.

Clare Kendrick began to think deliberately. Francis was being blackmailed. She knew she could help him but not yet how.

Kenneth Gibb arrived at the Foreign Office that morning still a little irritated. But he wasn't a man to allow irritation to impair expertise; he knew exactly what he would say to Menderez on the telephone: he would be friendly but with a hint, the barest hint of reserve. He knew just what he wanted and just how to do it. Really there were limits, and Menderez had overstepped them.

His hand was on the telephone when the instrument rang under it. Señor Menderez was in the waiting-room; he hadn't an appointment, he was apologizing, but ...

'Show him up at once, please.'

Menderez came in smiling. He smiled without the nuances, the nice variations in manner which to Kenneth Gibb were by now second nature; he smiled when he was amused, and privately Kenneth Gibb amused him. Menderez had a Christian name and *Señor* to preface it, but somehow nobody used either. He was Menderez – a character. He was small and taut with smooth black hair and a bright bird's eye. He sat before Gibb's desk, alert, vividly alive, a naked flame beside the other's guarded lamp.

'I'm afraid I rather let you down yesterday.'

'It's good of you to come and explain,' Gibb said. He was pleased with the sentence; he hadn't had time to consider it, and extempore he thought it rather good. It wasn't exactly reproof, but nor was it too easy acceptance ... Yes, it was professional.

'I was in a bit of a fix, you see, for I spoke too quickly when I agreed to see Mason at once. I can guess what he wants, and no doubt he told you in terms. What I realized I didn't know was how you stood yourself. So I had to put him off.'

'I'm not too sure I follow.'

'You've been in Candoro yourself, you know.'

'Certainly I have. And Candoro falls to this Department.'

'Yes, of course. You've a duty to Francis Mason, and naturally you'll perform it. I know all that – that's all tied up. What isn't so clear is your personal interest.'

'I do not have one,' Gibb said stiffly.

Menderez ignored this blandly. 'Then I must start at the beginning. ... Candoro is changing: you can't with impunity ride Presidents off your land. That affair was bad luck no doubt – bad luck on Clegg Mason that Romero should later be President – but really, he shouldn't have been doing that to any Candoran. Even six years ago. And now' – Menderez shrugged – 'the bird has returned to roost. It's likely to be an expensive fowl.'

'So I had gathered.'

'I'd give you a figure if I could. But I didn't come to talk

23

about that, for I thought you might have advised him not to pay at all.'

'Why should I do that – knowing Candoro?'

'Because you're not a fool,' Menderez said.

Kenneth Gibb thought rapidly. He knew what Menderez meant, but he couldn't decide whether it would be wise to concede it. He was a man who liked plenty of time to consider; he decided to temporize again. 'I'm out of my depth,' he said.

'Then I must swim to you.' Menderez's expression changed very slightly. 'I'm not very good at swimming.' He lit a cigarette, adding almost as narrative, as though it were commonly accepted: 'I give the Romeros six months. And you?'

'I couldn't possibly tell Romero's representative how long I thought he would survive.' Kenneth Gibb wasn't conscious that he was being pompous.

'In case I split on you, you mean?' Menderez looked at Gibb curiously. 'In any case,' he said finally, 'it wouldn't be correct.' He spoke with irony, but Gibb didn't notice it.

'I'm glad you understand.'

'Oh, of course. So let's leave it that it's my opinion – nobody else's – that Romero will last six months. . . . And afterwards, do you think?'

'God knows.'

'Perhaps. But I do.'

'Yes?'

'Yes. We shall be next. We – my party.'

'I didn't know you had one.'

'Of course you didn't. If I told you, you wouldn't believe me. No worthwhile member of my party ever admits it, or at any rate not in Candoro. Or the States for that matter. Only stooges have cards.'

Kenneth Gibb was seriously alarmed. Guilt by association, he thought. 'But –' he began.

'Oh, you needn't bother. I'm not a doctrinaire, you know. I'm not on the party line or anywhere near it, I expect I'll get shot in due course.'

'You're joking,' Gibb said. He was utterly outraged. Menderez was a career diplomatist. Gibb couldn't have been more scandalized if he had struck him; called him pederast. 'You're joking,' he said again.

24

'I leave you to guess how much.'

The ensuing silence didn't seem to embarrass Menderez; he went on smiling his amused, his amusing smile. Presently he said: 'We'll leave that, then. Back to the land, to Seven. Which may or mayn't be worth a bribe to Romero. It's a matter of opinion – an estimate of the Romeros' expectation of political life.'

'You could put it like that,' Gibb said. He was being very careful indeed.

'But you didn't say that to Mason?'

'No.'

'He didn't ask you?'

'Really, I ...'

'Oh, all right.' Menderez waved a hand. It was a small hand, muscular and very well cared for. 'The Masons have money in England,' he said casually; he was stating a fact. 'Bearer bonds.'

'Interesting,' Gibb said.

'Very. . . . Old Mason isn't deaf, is he?'

'Not that I know of.'

'Well, he was when he last left Candoro. He had a plug in his ear and a wire to a box. Quite a sizeable box. It was hung round his neck on a strap. Currency Control had an eye on him, but batteries for a hearing aid ...' Menderez chuckled. 'He's never used the thing again – that's how we tumbled. Bold as brass. Simple and so with a chance of success. It succeeded.'

'And no doubt quite illegal.'

'Oh, very.' Menderez straightened suddenly. 'We want that money,' he said shortly.

'Evidently.'

'So we don't want you airing the opinion that it might buy at most six months.'

'I haven't said that yet, but I may have to. I must advise as I ...'

Menderez interrupted. 'There's that job at NATO,' he said coolly.

'I don't know what you mean.'

For the first time Menderez showed impatience. 'Come off it,' he said crisply. 'Everybody in our curious profession knows about that job with NATO; everybody knows you're in the running. You'll need money for it, though – to make a success of it. You're not a rich man.'

'Really . . .'

Menderez said slowly, staring at Gibb: 'Lavinia Mason has substantial means.'

Kenneth Gibb's mouth opened and shut again. Faintly but unmistakably he began to gobble.

'I . . . I . . .'

Menderez ignored him; he seemed to be speaking to himself. 'Francis Mason,' he was saying. 'I rather like him, or I would if I allowed myself. But we'll have to carve him up.'

'Carve him up?' Gibb had managed speech again, but weakly.

'Yes. *We'll* take his money: *you* take his wife.'

'But . . .'

'And the job at NATO too. Which you certainly won't get if Sir Godfrey hears she's your mistress. Mistress – yes: the Office is reasonable. But wives of friends *en poste*, a house where you've stayed . . .' Menderez shook his head. 'No,' he said decisively. He rose with an equal decision. 'We're agreed?'

Kenneth Gibb was silent, fiddling with his tie.

'I really think we must be.' Menderez walked to the door, turning at it unexpectedly. His face was expressionless but his voice precise. 'And don't double-cross me,' he said. 'God help you if you do.'

He began to walk to his flat. He was a man who enjoyed exercise and in London missed it. He had been born in Candoro, and far up-country, on an *estancia* which had been in his family even longer than had Seven in the Masons'. His blood was the purest Spanish, though he wasn't particularly proud of it. What he was proud of was Candoro.

Which he now had to serve, he thought, and not as a first secretary. He and a handful of others. And by no means the handful which Gibb, much too promptly, had supposed.

He laughed aloud. It had been amusing to tease Kenneth Gibb, and how he had scared him! He had thought he was a Commie; he couldn't have been more frightened if he'd appeared through the floor – loud bang, forked tail swishing, strong smell of brimstone. It didn't do for up-and-coming young diplomatists to mix with Communists, except official ones, and Kenneth Gibb well knew it. Not that he, Menderez, hadn't deliberately misled him.

And not wholly in mischief, for he had had in mind a calculated deception.

For there was trouble in Candoro and much of it. The Romeros had gone too far. They were in fact rather old-fashioned as political scoundrels went, for they had none of the connexions with an industrial class which, somewhat to the south, had kept more subtle parvenus in power for years. Nor had they inherited huge wartime reserves of foreign exchange, spending them on maintaining themselves. Condoro, very small in any case, hadn't profiteered quite shamelessly. Their neighbours regarded Candorans as thirty years behind the times, and to this Candorans were sensitive. But they preferred their own ways. They weren't, by and large, a politically minded people. In summer it was much too hot, and in winter never too severe, there was work, a man's family, an excellent local wine. Kenneth Gibb had been right when he had said that in Candoro, provided you paid your taxes, minded your own business and kept your mouth shut, nothing very dreadful happened to you.

But for the few who didn't, those like himself who cared ... Menderez's expression hardened. The Romeros might have come to power by an old-fashioned gun-fight in the capital, but they hadn't stayed old-fashioned; they had learnt very quickly and from hideous sources. Their techniques, by the standards of those sources, were very contemporary indeed.

Their collapse wasn't something which worried Menderez. He longed for it passionately. What worried him was what would replace them.

It mightn't be Candoran at all.

He weighed the chances for the hundredth time as he walked to his flat. What he feared was Communism. In Candoro it was very well-organized. It had to be, for the Romeros by now were efficient. Plenty of people depended on them – the secret police, for instance. Many would die in any night of the long knives. But it had paid him to mislead Kenneth Gibb, to hint that he was a Communist, for Gibb would at once discount him. There was a great Power to the north which didn't approve of Communism. Look what had happened in that banana republic. Great Powers talked of non-intervention, mouthing the words unctuously, but when it came to important interests, fruit, for instance, a major investment ... And Candoro was in South America.

'... My very dear chap, they wouldn't last a month. How
27

could they when the Americans wouldn't stand for it? Cannot. Dare not. . . .'

Menderez could hear Gibb saying it.

He knew the argument; knew that it wasn't silly. But he didn't accept it, for he had very good reason not to: he had Communist contacts and the highest imaginable respect for them. He was playing the most dangerous game in the world, trying to use Communism. It was lethal and he knew it. He was a patriot, mentally and emotionally committed, but he wasn't a romantic; he knew too that his own friends were quite unorganized – a few old families like his own, an official or two, boys at the two ancient universities. Not even the army, for Romero was good to the army. They hadn't a hope in hell. But somehow capture the other machine, master it, use it . . .

Probably it was impossible, and certainly it was dangerous. It had never been done – always it had been the reverse. And if they caught you at it . . .

Menderez smiled grimly.

I'm a fool, he reflected, but a Candoran fool. I haven't an option. It was Romero or Communism. Leave Romero, do nothing, and the other was inevitable. He knew it, knew its power, its immaculate organization. People like Kenneth Gibb weighed the political forces and perhaps assessed them rightly. They knew nothing of the men and women concerned, the cells, the ceaseless work, the tight priest-like loyalties.

He came to his flat and went in. And we shall have to be very quick, he thought, undressing. Money and arms we need, but money first. Say fifty thousand pounds. But money. What that Excellency rumpot thinks he can get from the Masons.

And if you were discovered at it . . .

Things would start happening.

As in fact they had. Mr Peter Amadeus was sitting in his finely furnished study talking to a beautiful young man. Amadeus himself had a large bald head on a neck too long for it. He did what he could about that, wearing collars very cunningly cut, but his shoulders, narrow and sloping, defeated him. Even in his beautifully made collars the simile of a tortoise was inescapable. His skin was as white as a woman's, and his mouth, small and pouting, very red. His hands were a little fleshy, but his grip was firm. He smiled a lot, showing good teeth but not his own.

He was a remarkable man. An organization called the Security Executive, its head in particular, would have given its eyes to know just a little more than it did – just enough to make a case before a court. But they had almost despaired, for in his profession Amadeus was exceptional. The police had nothing against him: he wasn't police business. But those who weren't exactly policemen, the Security Executive for instance, had him high on their secret records He was what for want of a better word they listed as an agent, but he was something more – a superlative organizer. Scarcely a piece of skullduggery, high-level international skullduggery, could not be linked with Amadeus. Linked but never proved. Though there was a Power which would gladly have accredited him he wasn't a diplomat, for diplomats could always be got rid of. At a pinch a diplomat could always be declared *non grata*. So that formal immunity Amadeus despised since protection he had himself organized – widespread, beautifully knit protection. He worked on the simplest of principles: get something on the men who counted. Then you could do almost as you pleased. It was astonishing how most of the men who counted had something to hide. Politicians, prelates, newspaper proprietors, the men who denied they were powerful but were, the faceless men of Whitehall.

Mr Peter Amadeus knew it. He was conscious that this was power. Not overt power, not power in the fancy dresses which the English loved, but power both certain and immediately applicable.

Peter Amadeus applied it. He was rich now, but he didn't work for riches; he worked for love – love of his profession and a contempt for men. It had never ceased to astonish him that in Anglo-Saxon communities sex should be taken so seriously. Every sort of sex. To Peter Amadeus sex was a prime tool of his trade.

He was saying to the young man a trifle petulantly: 'Our unpredictable employers ... But thorough. The latest they give me is that Romero is blackmailing an Anglo-Candoran family called Mason. These Masons have money in England and, since the asset is within my jurisdiction, I was told about it.' Like many superior lawbreakers Amadeus had a weakness for legal language. He stroked his considerable jowl before he added: 'Now what am I supposed to do with that?'

The young man ran a hand through curling hair. Once it had been straight, but that had been before success in either of his professions. 'Nothing,' he said.

'I'm glad you agree. Money alone wouldn't prop Romero; moreover he may be intending to leave it here.' Amadeus chuckled. 'Another foreign nest-egg against the inevitable. And in any case one of these Masons, Francis Mason, is over here negotiating. That means negotiating with the Candoran embassy, and in the Candoran embassy sits our excellent friend Menderez. If this were conceivably anything but a private Romero killing, Menderez would tell us.'

The young man said quietly: 'Would he?'

Amadeus looked at him sharply. 'I can understand you don't like him. He's hardly your cup.'

'It isn't that. . . . We know very little about him, really.'

'He's not on the formal strength, if that's what you mean. Why should he be? Thousands aren't, and that includes most of the best ones. Justification by works, you know – rather a grand phrase for fellow traveller.'

'I admit he's helped us. Nothing major, perhaps, but by no means negligible.'

'Then what are you fussed about? It'll be a trifling sum in any case – a mere personal fortune.' Amadeus waved a manicured hand. 'To our masters that sort of money is nothing.'

'Oh, yes. But Candoro is getting pretty warm – pretty near a crisis. It's a principle to minimize risks.'

'Risks which you can't define?'

'I don't attempt to.'

'Then what are you suggesting?'

'Nothing melodramatic – I loathe melodrama. But we might do a little discreet verification. Of Menderez's contacts, for instance, particularly his Candoran ones.'

Amadeus shrugged. 'All right,' he said. 'It can't do any harm.'

CHAPTER FOUR

IN a room in the Foreign Office a good deal grander than Kenneth Gibb's, Kenneth Gibb was being discussed. The room belonged to Sir Godfrey Henn, and he was talking to William Lampe-Lister. Sir Godfrey was what was called a Deputy Under Secretary of State and William Lampe-Lister an Assistant Under Secretary. They were very important persons, though nobody would have guessed it from their manner or appearance. Sir Godfrey was bland and untidy and Irish; and supremely shrewd. Lampe-Lister, a little younger, was the world's best listener; he wasn't less shrewd than Sir Godfrey, but he had had a year or two less service to be shrewd in. Sir Godfrey was called Gog, William Lampe-Lister Magog, for they were very old friends indeed.

Gog was looking at three files on the desk before him. 'Peterson and Smith and Gibb,' he was saying.

'It's a damned important job. We've got to choose right.'

'Of course we have.' Sir Godfrey tapped his files. 'I suggest we eliminate. Peterson and Smith – they're not quite ... quite ripe.'

'Given half a dozen first-class candidates I'd agree with you.'

'Which we don't have.'

'Precisely. So that if you eliminate Smith and Peterson you're left with Gibb.'

'Whom you don't much like.'

'I didn't say that,' Magog said coolly.

'I know you didn't, William. But I also know you don't much care for him.'

'He's an admirable official. Up to a point.'

'He's got brains.'

'So have dozens.'

Sir Godfrey chuckled, 'I think you'd better talk.'

'If I must. .... I don't want to be unfair, but I've never got out of my head that he didn't fight. I know that not every young Englishman with an excellent job abroad rushed home to enlist, but I'm blimp enough to prefer the ones who did.'

'He was in Rio, wasn't he?'

'Yes. One of the big chemical firms. He was a technician then.'

'He'd only have been eighteen in thirty-nine. A boy.'

'No doubt. And nineteen-thirty-nine wasn't particularly rousing. But he was twenty-one in forty-two . . . and still in Rio.'

'Going great guns,' Gog said.

'Indeed he was. He wasn't a technician any longer; he was going up the ladder.'

'We took him on next year, I think.'

'And very glad to get him. We were desperate – desperate for local staff. His firm didn't like it, but they were rather flattered too.'

'When did we make him permanent?'

'Early in forty-six.'

'Hm. . . .' Sir Godfrey shook his untidy head. '*Not* a vintage year. We'd had years without regular recruitment and we lost our heads. We made far too many mistakes. Look at that economist fellow. He was first class in London – wonderful on paper and talked to a Minister perfectly. And the first job we give him abroad, the first time the heat goes on, he falls to pieces. Where is he now, by the way?'

'In a Home.'

Sir Godfrey lit a cigarette from a tattered packet of twenty; he stuffed the packet carelessly back into his pocket. '*Not* a vintage year,' he repeated. 'We took too many and too soon.'

'Whereby', Magog said slowly, 'there's now a promotion block half a mile long.'

'And the man who gets this NATO job will be through it? Finally. On his way in fact.'

'Exactly.'

'I agree we've got to be careful – very careful. But Gibb isn't just one of the bright temporaries we established on too little evidence. *He* didn't break down abroad. Look at the record.' Gog read from the file before him. 'Temporary service in Rio de Janeiro. Established nineteen-forty-six. Spell in the Office here to get the hang of it. Posting to Rome – you go wrong in Rome if you're going wrong anywhere – then off to Candoro. Excellent reports everywhere. Back to the Office again from Candoro and promoted one rung two years ago. That wasn't so easy, you know: fifty-eight wasn't forty-six – we weren't making fools of ourselves in fifty-eight. The right sort of background, too, which means today that it wasn't a foolishly expensive one. That's one lesson we've learned, at any rate. Me, I welcome it.'

'He'll need money in Paris, though. Lots of it.'

Sir Godfrey consulted his files again. 'I agree the allowance is only fair. We'll have to get the inspectors to do one of their little Reports. They're very good at them – more than a match for the Treasury. But I admit it takes time.'

Magog stroked his chin before he said thoughtfully: 'You mustn't think I've anything against him because he isn't the conventional idea of a diplomat. All that is very old hat.'

'William, come clean.' Gog was smiling.

William Lampe-Lister considered, staring from the window at the debased-Palladian courtyard. After some time he said: 'I don't like his smell.'

'Oh come. He's got something.'

'And something he hasn't.'

Sir Godfrey Henn was silent for a very long time, his level inspection of Magog not wavering. Finally he said: 'William, I've known you a great many years. The record – the evidence – is flat against you. But I don't remember when last you were wrong. We'll hold it; we'll keep decision for a fortnight. We can manage that, I think.'

'Just about,' Magog said.

It was characteristic of Clare Kendrick that she had taken both her decisions together. She had decided to find out what would most help Francis Mason, the price which Romero would accept to take the heat off; and she had decided to give that information to Francis. A woman less honest with herself might have taken the first, dallying with the second; playing with it; looking at and around it. That would have been easy, for after all it wasn't so terribly simple to acquire information which, by your official rank, you hadn't any right to. Passing it on was the impropriety. Clare would have admitted this, and quite without cynicism. Improper it was, and impropriety the odious noun. At most she would have pleaded that it was a very male one. She, Clare Kendrick, was in love.

She had made her plan carefully, and it wasn't a bad one. The information, the figure acceptable, would be in the ambassador's room, and it was unlikely to be amongst his personal papers. Dickie Romero was notoriously careless, but he wasn't as careless as that. It would be a private letter probably, or perhaps a note of some telephone conversation between brother and brother. They were always telephoning, and the ambassador was always making notes. There was a very fair chance that what she wanted existed.

In the safe.

For she knew that carelessness with papers, at first sight her ally, was in fact against her. What was against her was the archivist. That was what he was called, but Clare was aware that he was in fact the Security Officer. He had been put there by the senior Romero when his brother's habits could no longer be accepted, and he was very good at his job. He locked the ambassador's papers when he left his room; sometimes he even kept him sober. Not that the latter duty was particularly important: everybody knew that Dickie Romero was Romero's brother; everybody knew that he wasn't, in the usual sense, ambassador at all. He was a mountebank, a playboy, but he was a President's brother. There was a vague counsellor somewhere, but Gibb hadn't exaggerated when he had told Francis Mason that in practice Menderez ran the embassy. But Clare didn't think that what she wanted would be with Menderez. Menderez was a career diplomatist, a professional; but this was family business, a family killing.

That decision taken, the archivist was the key – and literally. He was Dickie Romero's shadow, something between a keeper and a nurse. The ambassador apart, he alone knew the combination to the safe in the ambassador's room. He had a room of his own downstairs and he seldom left it. In any case it was a combination.

A woman more experienced would probably have trusted luck, waiting till His Excellency was drunk again, his papers strewn about him; coming in on some excuse or other; chancing her stars. Clare's plan was more precise. It was Friday and there was a Report to finish. What more natural than to work late instead of dragging into the office on a Saturday? So far so good – there was nothing suspicious in that. But access to the papers she had still to contrive, and only the archivist could give it her. Very well, she would *ask* for it. There were figures which she needed for the Report she was working on, confidential figures, but not so confidential that a Confidential Secretary wasn't entitled to them. That was the plan as far as it went. ... Confidential Secretary working late and quite unsuspiciously. Confidential Secretary wants confidential figures. Asks archivist to open the safe for her. Goes up with him and he opens it.

... Archivist called away.

She had planned it carefully. She had made an engagement with a girl friend, but it wasn't quite a firm one. She might be kept late, she had said. If Mary would ring at five to seven precisely ...

Mary was very dull, and Clare hadn't fancied an evening with her; but she was also extremely reliable. If she said she would ring at five to seven she would ring at five to seven exactly.

When the safe would be open, the archivist at Clare's shoulder. There would be nobody else in the office. Of course it might not work: the archivist might let the telephone ring out; he might ask her to answer it herself; he might shut the safe before he left. He might, he might ...

It was an innocent little plan, but it wasn't a stupid one. A professional could have improved on it, but not, within its limits, greatly.

Now Clare was counting the minutes till a quarter to seven; then she went down to the archivist. He looked at the clock a little surlily. 'You're pretty late,' he said in Spanish.

'I must finish that Report.'

She told him what she wanted, and he rose without comment. They went upstairs to the ambassador's room. Clare looked at her watch. ...

Seven minutes to seven.

The archivist turned the dials, the tumblers clicking faintly. He was maddeningly slow about it. It was with Mary now, Mary and some nameless girl in an exchange. If it came through too quickly, or more than a minute late ...

Clare Kendrick stood perfectly still. He mustn't *smell* me, he mustn't smell fear. ...

In the basement the telephone rang sharply.

The archivist grunted. His fingers left the dials and he straightened his back. He left the room without a word.

The safe was shut still.

Casually, not thinking, Clare touched the handle.

The door swung deliberately open. Very slowly she put her hand out.

Another fell lightly on her shoulder and she froze at once. 'Can I help you?' Menderez was asking. His voice was cool.

'What are you doing here?' She knew the question was absurd.

'I might ask you the same.'

'I'm finishing that Report.'

'Up here?'

'I wanted some figures, so . . .'

'I see,' he said. She was conscious he didn't believe her.

The archivist returned, his jaw dropping at the open safe. He turned furiously on Clare, but Menderez spoke first. 'You fool,' he said concisely.

'What do you mean?'

'You're never to leave that safe open. It's what you're for.'

'I didn't. I . . . She . . .'

'But you did. I don't know whether you knew it, and I don't care. But what you'd done was to complete the combination. . . . And you left the room.' Menderez was very severe.

'I assure you . . . Anyway, why did she touch it?' The archivist had a point; he was hitting back.

'Because she's security-minded. More so than you.'

'But . . .'

Menderez paid no attention. 'Don't you see what you've done, man? That safe was open – open, you hear me? It was open and you didn't know it. If she hadn't tried the handle, what would have happened? Suppose you'd been kept downstairs; suppose she'd decided not to wait for you. Would you have checked it before you left? A safe you thought shut?' Menderez was getting quite angry; he answered his own rhetoric. 'No,' he said decisively, 'you would not. Why should you? You'd have simply gone home. And His Excellency's safe would have been open to anybody who came in. The cleaners probably – they arrive first in the morning. What do you know about the cleaners?'

'Sir,' the archivist said. '*Señor* . . .'

'Or His Excellency could have discovered it himself. And what do you think would happen then?'

The archivist was silent.

'It's really my duty to tell him.'

'*Señor*, Your Excellency . . .'

'But I won't. I know you've a family,' Menderez added. 'In Candoro.'

36

The archivist bowed.

'You can go now. I'll shut that thing later.'

'I think I'll do it myself.'

The archivist crossed to the safe, shutting the door and spinning the dials again, carefully, first left, then right; he bowed again and left them. They could hear his footsteps diminishing down the stairs.

Menderez laughed shortly on a note Clare hadn't heard. 'Well,' he said amazingly, 'we nearly brought it off. Between us.'

Clare stared at him.

He smiled at her, pulling an armchair to the ambassador's desk, handing her into it, sitting at the desk himself. 'Now the truth, please.' But his voice was friendly, the tone one of polite conversation.

'I . . .'

'Perhaps that was a little abrupt. I'll have to help you.' They had dropped into Spanish again. Menderez put two beautiful shoes on His Excellency's desk, tilting his chair. 'It is possible we were after the same thing,' he said slowly.

Clare was silent, and Menderez put his feet down; he leant forward, solemn now, but still not angry. 'You're in love with him, aren't you?' he asked.

His gentleness rather than the question almost broke her. Anger she could have faced, or the official manner, but Menderez showed neither. He wasn't cross or even shocked; in a fashion she could sense he was her friend. It was wholly unexpected and she was very young. But she saw that it would be futile to pretend. 'Yes,' she said presently.

He leant forward again, perfectly relaxed. 'You were talking about figures – I think that was half the truth. Not figures but a figure. Francis Mason . . .'

She nodded dumbly.

'I wish I knew too. What they would accept, I mean.

'You don't?'

'I do not. I came to find out.'

'But the safe . . .?'

He chuckled. 'I haven't your ingenuity, Clare. Nor your guts. Nor your motive. I'd written off the safe. But I've a key to the cabinets. I thought it worth a shot.' He frowned for an instant, considering. 'Run down for a moment,' he said. 'See whether the archivist has gone.'

She came back at once. 'He's left.'

'I don't blame him in the least – he probably needs a drink. A fifty to one chance. He's a good man too – that sort of chance always picks the good ones. Anyway, he's shut the safe and gone. He knows I've a key to the cabinets.'

For half an hour they rummaged, then Menderez locked up again methodically. 'No go,' he said. 'I didn't really hope.' He sat down once more at the ambassador's desk. Now he was very still.

'Shall I make you some tea?'

He accepted, not moving, erect in his chair as Clare busied herself in the outer office. He was evidently thinking. But over tea he was at ease again. They drank cosily, almost in intimacy. At last he said: 'I know your motive, or I think I do. It's very – very irregular.'

'I suppose so.'

'But extremely human. It's wrong, but it doesn't offend me.'

'You're very understanding.'

Menderez waved a hand. 'It's rather a meaningless word. .... So I've guessed your motive, but I don't think you know mine.'

'I'm sure I don't.'

'Then I'll tell you. It's pique – sheer professional pique. I've been told what's in the wind, and my instructions are to work on Francis Mason – to give him the run around and to soften him up. Our lamentable superior keeps the rest to himself. He'll come in when it's time to – after I've done the dirty. And I don't like that. I'm a professional diplomat, and the ambassador's a wastrel. I won't be pushed around; I won't just be used.'

She inspected him unflinchingly, saying very softly: 'You were talking about half-truths.'

He took it without emotion. 'So I was.'

'The whole is better.'

'Sometimes.' He looked at her quickly, taut and aware. They were very alike in their intense vitality. He's very attractive, she was thinking, very much a man. If it wasn't for Francis ...

Menderez lit a cigarette, blowing the smoke carefully away from Clare, for he knew she disliked it. Suddenly he said: 'You don't want Mason skinned, of course.'

'Of course I don't.'

'I don't mind that myself. I don't mind his paying to Candoro what I conceive he owes it.'

'But the Romeros aren't Candoro.

He looked at her steadily, not answering. But she pressed him. 'Then why ...?'

Smiling, he held his hand up. 'Let's leave it', he said slowly, 'that I'm not exactly *for* them.' He looked at her again before he added: 'Can you reach Francis Mason?'

She nodded unhappily, uncertain.

'Tonight?'

'I can try.'

'Please ring him, then. Ask him to see me tomorrow morning.'

Francis Mason hadn't been surprised when at half past twelve Kenneth Gibb had telephoned postponing their lunch together. There was nothing from the embassy still : it hadn't been Francis's morning and he was ready to accept that it wasn't going to be his day. He listened to Gibb with a certain fatalism; he had almost rung off before he realized that Kenneth Gibb was inviting him to dinner instead. That evening. And there was an urgency in his carefully casual phrases, something which the telephone couldn't quite obliterate. Francis caught it precisely. Kenneth Gibb wasn't simply being polite; Kenneth Gibb wanted to see Francis Mason. 'I'd like to,' he said. 'Thank you.'

'Come to my club.'

'All right.'

'At eight, shall we say?'

'At eight, then.'

Francis replaced the receiver; he was frowning, for he was in a difficulty. He had promised to take Lavinia to a theatre, and now he must disappoint her. It was business, of course – what he had come to London for. A sensible woman must realize that, a sensible woman would agree at once. Nevertheless he wasn't happy.

He found his wife in her room, resting on the bed. She didn't trouble to remove her face-pack. 'I'm afraid I must disappoint you this evening,' he said.

She didn't answer him.

'It's business, naturally, or I wouldn't be letting you down. I was lunching with Kenneth Gibb, but he's had to put me off. It's dinner instead, I'm afraid. I'll have to go.'

'Business,' she said.

'I'm free for the afternoon, though. You wouldn't like a matinée instead?'

'Nobody,' Lavinia said, 'nobody goes to matinées.' Her manner dismissed all matinées.

'I'm very sorry.'

'You must do what you have to. . . . Of course.'

He left the room, frowning still, lunching alone in the restaurant of the hotel. The afternoon he spent at the matinée which Lavinia had declined and, after a drink in a bar, walked slowly to Gibb's club.

Kenneth Gibb had been careful about his club. He hadn't joined the first which he could have, nor was he interested in what, though never publicly, he would have called mere social values. There were clubs West of his own where the members were a good deal grander, and later, when he was getting near the top, it might not be unwise to join one. Not now, though. The aura, the smell of his Service was changing: the latest snobbery was anti-snobbery. It didn't do even to risk the impression that you might be climbing. The seniors, the real Big Men, disliked it. What you wanted was a decent sort of place where you met your own kind, men out of the ruck admittedly, but men still moving. Later perhaps . . .

In his judiciously chosen club Kenneth Gibb was waiting for Francis Mason. Francis had been right in thinking that when Gibb had telephoned in the morning an unusual urgency had leaked along the line. Gibb as it happened had been both angry and, though he hadn't had time to define the emotion, a little frightened. The anger had been at a personal affront – Menderez was threatening him; and the fright at the thought, the bare possibility of blackmail. Menderez was trying to blackmail him – him, Kenneth Gibb.

But by now he had had time to consider, and he had more than three-quarters reassured himself. After all it was only Menderez: everybody knew about Menderez. He was a career diplomatist, but he didn't behave like one. He knew people he shouldn't or at least needn't, people who couldn't possibly advance his career;

and he was appallingly outspoken – a freak, a sport. Menderez needn't be taken very seriously.

And Gibb had asked himself what Menderez was in fact pressing him to do, deciding that it was to give advice which in any case he would have given. It was clear that Romero was pursuing the Masons, and relentlessly. Money alone might buy him off. But that was what he had already said when Mason had first come to see him. Romero could fall, no doubt, but when was anybody's guess. And anybody's risk. Anybody's but Kenneth Gibb's. Suppose he advised Francis Mason to wait and, a week or two later, the *estancia* went up in flames? That couldn't be ruled out.

No, he couldn't take the risk. This wasn't a defeat – certainly not one by Menderez. If blackmail had been intended the threat was a hollow one. He was doing no more than he would have.

Kenneth Gibb had always been able to convince himself quite easily.

Perfectly collected now, he was in the smoking-room when the porter brought Francis in. He rose at once. 'I'm sorry to have put you off.'

'Not at all.'

Gibb ordered drinks and they drank them quietly. 'What happened this morning was that Menderez came to see me, and he kept me too late to lunch with you. Besides, I had to think about it.' Kenneth Gibb paused, but if he had expected a question Francis disappointed him. Presently he went on again. 'Menderez asked me to tell you he was sorry he had let you down.' This was true only by inference, but Gibb said it smoothly. 'He was in a bit of a fix, or thought he was.'

'*He* was in a fix?'

'So he seemed to think. He's not a bad negotiator' – Francis caught a hint of patronage – 'and like all good negotiators he likes to know where he stands before he starts.'

'I'd have thought that was clear,' Mason said.

'Not quite.'

'I'm afraid I don't follow.'

Kenneth Gibb smiled his most professional smile. 'It isn't quite bilateral,' he said, 'not wholly between you and Menderez.'

'I don't see anybody else in it.'

'Well . . . There's myself.'

Francis shook his head.

41

'It's simple, really. You came to us for advice, and Menderez wanted to know what advice we'd given you.'

'Good God! He's got a nerve.'

'He has indeed. Naturally I didn't tell him.'

'Come to that,' Francis said slowly, 'there was nothing to tell him. You haven't advised me yet – not in terms.'

'You're asking me to? Now?'

'I am.'

Kenneth Gibb, conscious of the gesture, beckoned to a waiter. The timing, he was thinking, wasn't ineffective. Things like that were important – expert. The waiter brought drinks again, and Gibb raised his slowly. 'Your very good health,' he said. 'I'm afraid you're going to need it.'

'Meaning?'

'That they have you by the short hairs.'

'I know it.'

'I think you should settle – make the best terms you can.'

'He didn't talk money? He gave you no hint of a price?'

'I'm afraid there's a lot before that,' Gibb said. 'Candorans ...' His shrug was very well done.

'But where should I start?'

'At the beginning. Let him see you'll pay. Something.'

'He must know that already or I wouldn't be here.'

'I agree. But there's a form in these things, you know. Make the concession formally – in principle. Let him see for certain that you'll play. Move from there.' Gibb rose a little unexpectedly. 'Keep me in touch, of course – perhaps I can help again later. Now let's have dinner.'

FRANCIS MASON did not see Clare next morning when he called at the Candoran embassy, for he was shown directly to Menderez's room. Menderez rose to meet him. 'We've met before,' he said.

Francis politely inspected him. 'I know your face,' he said at last. It was perfectly true. 'But I can't place it.'

Menderez laughed. 'I'm sorry you won that race – I wanted it very badly. But your horse was much the better animal.'

'I remember now.'

They chatted for some time, Francis relaxing, talking of the interests common to up-country Candorans, of cattle, shooting, and of little race meetings. Menderez did it beautifully. He was a diplomat, but he didn't, like Kenneth Gibb, constantly remind himself of the techniques of his profession. He didn't need to, for he had something more valuable than any technique and, in the pinches, much more effective; he had natural good manners and an ease with men. Presently he said: 'But I'm afraid I didn't ask you here to talk about anything as pleasant as the life we live in Candoro.' His expression changed, but not unpleasantly. 'Or used to,' he added.

'I realize that.'

'Then let me say I think you've had bad luck. There are 100,000 Candorans your grandfather could have ridden off Seven with impunity. Not that I approve the action, naturally: it was rude and arbitrary, and if he had got away with it, that's a criticism of Candoro as it was. But it was plain bad luck that he picked a man who later became President.'

'Thank you. You make it sound almost reasonable.'

Menderez smiled, but for a moment dropped his eyes. Not raising them he said deliberately: 'I work for the Romeros because I must. Let's leave it at that. But I work for them.'

'I think I understand.'

'Then you'll also understand that they've reason not to like you.'

'They've made that clear enough.' Francis Mason sounded grim.

'And you know how Candoro is run? As it is, I mean?'

'I'm a Candoran too.'

'Good. Then we start on common ground. ... They'll want money, of course.'

'I know that too. What I don't know is what it will buy.'

'I'm not sure I'm with you.'

Francis said wryly: 'I'm British by blood, but I said I was also Candoran. I meant it. It's my country in a sense it isn't grandfather's. I'm not active in politics but I follow them. And I don't believe the Romeros can last much longer.'

'I see,' Menderez said slowly. He was thinking that some people – that Kenneth Gibb, for instance – considered Francis Mason something of a simpleton.

They might have to think again.

He considered for a moment, then said evenly: 'I can hardly advise you, you know.'

'I suppose not. But you can see that we're in a bigger jam than the mere fact that Romero has the heat on us. We're *estancia*-owners – by Candoran standards rich. Romero apart, we're not exactly popular. In a sense we're an anachronism ... So we buy off Romero, and he falls. And then?'

Very quietly, not moving, Menderez asked: 'What is it you fear?'

'Sequestration,' Francis said.

The long silence which followed was broken by the telephone on Menderez's desk. He answered politely but shortly. 'I'll ring you back, if I may.' He returned to Francis Mason. 'That was Kenneth Gibb,' he explained; he offered a cigarette. 'Do you like him?' he asked unexpectedly.

'Well ...'

'I don't actively dislike him, or not yet. But I think he's an ass.'

Francis laughed. 'He's certainly very correct.'

'Correct – yes, very. But I sometimes wonder how he'd act in a situation where correctitude wasn't the test of conduct – where the rules weren't in the book.' Menderez dismissed Kenneth Gibb with a wave of his beautiful hand. 'But we were talking about sequestration. Who do you think would seize Seven?'

'You know as well as I.'

'You think they could come to power?'

'It's possible.'

'I am against them,' Menderez said coolly. '*We* are against them.'

'But who is we?'

'Most of Candoro still.'

'Which isn't politically organized?'

'Admittedly.'

'Whereas they are?'

'I'm afraid so.'

'So that it comes to this: you're asking me to buy off Romero, but you can't guarantee – you won't even advise – that if we do we shan't be wasting our money.'

Menderez chuckled. He liked a fighter, and Francis Mason struck him as a promising one. That wasn't his reputation; he was supposed to be retiring, rather mild. Well, reputation was a bubble. At bottom he was vintage Mason. 'You haven't the option,' he said pleasantly.

'Why not?'

'You live on Seven. Seven is you.'

'Not quite. You know as well as I do that we couldn't pay Romero by selling off bits of the *estancia*. It would be fatal, that. So if we can pay him at all we must have something outside.'

'We know you have. Most ingenious it was, and – '

But Francis interrupted. 'And if we have anything worth mentioning outside we could live on it. We could even start elsewhere.'

But Menderez shook his head. 'No,' he said with decision. 'You're Seven. Seven has you.'

'Four generations, you mean? I admit it's something. We're not rootless. My grandfather . . .'

'It would break his heart.'

'You're closer than you think.' For a moment Francis hesitated; then he said slowly: 'Did you know he had angina?'

'I didn't. I'm sorry.'

'You needn't be too sorry. He's had a wonderful life. I don't think he wants to die slowly.'

'I'm quite sure of that.' Menderez considered again. 'I can see you have a card,' he said.

'A sort of card. I can't just bang it down, though. *I* might leave Seven, and when Granclegg dies I could. But not while he lives.

45

And I can't stall indefinitely in case he dies, for things could happen meanwhile. In Candoro, I mean, and on Seven.'

'They could indeed.'

'Well, you see how it stands.' Francis was silent for some time; at last he said: 'Nevertheless I'm authorized to bargain.'

'Make me an offer,' Menderez said.

'How much do you want?'

'How much have you got?'

Francis Mason's serious face broke unaffectedly. 'You can't think I'd tell you that.'

'I don't really.'

'Then you start *me*.'

'Well ... Five thousand they asked for the bridge, I believe – five thousand a year. Say ten years' purchase: Fifty thousand pounds.'

'That would be crippling.'

'So would be no bridge.'

Francis couldn't help laughing; he was liking Menderez. 'I'll make it ten,' he said.

'I can tell you that wouldn't be enough.'

'I might agree ... if the time factor wasn't so uncertain.'

'That's hardly an argument we can put to Romero.'

'I see that, naturally. But you must realize it weighs with us.'

'Of course I do. You're buying blind. I can't deny that. I don't.'

'Well then ...'

'I'd put it forward,' Menderez began, 'but ...'

'But what?'

'It isn't only the bridge, you know. Romero's an impatient man.'

'Also a conceited one.'

Menderez didn't answer, but he didn't protest.

'And susceptible to insult – real or imagined.'

'Just so.'

'Which ten thousand pounds might seem?'

'You're a pleasure to do business with.'

'And impatient men can act – well, impatiently?'

'I'm glad you see that.'

'Make it fifteen,' Francis said.

'I daren't.'

'I'm sorry, then.'

Menderez rose. 'I don't think we'll get farther today.' For a moment he waited before, almost shyly, he asked: 'Would you accept an invitation?'

'To this embassy?'

'Yes.'

'Of course. It's my own.'

Menderez smiled again. 'Excellent,' he said. 'Then there's a party here tonight as it happens – cocktails if you drink them, wine if you don't. I'm afraid it's very short notice, but would you come? And your wife if she hasn't an engagement?'

'We'd like to.'

'There'll be one or two you know. A few Candorans, but mostly the diplomats. Kenneth Gibb –'

'Kenneth Gibb again?'

'You needn't talk to him.'

They laughed simultaneously and Menderez shook hands. A servant, very stately, showed Francis out. He began to walk back to his hotel. He was shaking his head, for he was puzzled. It had gone much as he had expected, but somehow it hadn't. Menderez was working for Romero, but Menderez himself, the man ...

There was a card out somewhere.

In his room in the Foreign Office Kenneth Gibb was thinking. He had telephoned to Menderez on something of an impulse, for he had wanted confirmation of an opinion which he had half-realized Menderez was unlikely to give him formally. Gibb wasn't a man who normally acted on impulse, and now he was glad that Menderez had been engaged. When he rang back – *if* he rang back – he, Kenneth Gibb, would ask him something else, something routine and innocuous.

Nevertheless he would have been happy to pick Menderez's brains, for it might have solved his problem, or at least have given him a line on it.

The problem had nothing to do with Francis Mason, but was how to write his quarterly report on Candoro - what attitude to take, what flavour it should carry to his superiors. It was quite an important task and, for a man wildly ambitious, a very important one. It wasn't something which would simply go on file: a Deputy Under Secretary of State would see it and a junior

Minister. If Candoro got hot the Secretary of State for Foreign Affairs would ask for it himself – that and the latest dispatches from Her Majesty's ambassador upon which, but only partly, Gibb's report would have been based. They would be his bible, his terms of reference.

Kenneth Gibb took great trouble with these quarterly summaries, and he had been working on this one for three weeks. It lay on the desk before him now, for he had put it away for a week in order to come fresh to its final revision. And now he was uncertain about it, undecided about its tone.

He wouldn't have admitted it, but in fact he was uncertain about its timing.

For it had been one of the most definite reports he had ever written. Even allowing for the natural caution, the circumlocution of any public servant, it had committed him to the view that the régime of the Romeros couldn't last much longer.

And now he was wondering about that, or rather trying to decide whether this was the time to say so. There was so much to lose. There was that job at NATO ... Put in a definite report, come down positively on one side of the fence, and, if you chose the wrong one, it would certainly be noticed. And to your detriment. But stay on the fence and nobody would particularly blame you that you hadn't guessed right. After all, the Foreign Service was a service, and in any service you were judged not by the number of your successes but by the absence of your failures.

This wasn't the moment to risk a mistake.

Kenneth Gibb wasn't considering Francis Mason as he drew his report towards him, far less the advice he had given him. He was considering Kenneth Gibb. A brilliant success might help him – might, he decided, but not very much, for nobody thanked you for brilliantly forecasting what inevitably would be unwelcome. Whereas if you were wrong, he could see the raised eyebrows, the polite disapproval on the floors above him, the thought, never expressed, that Kenneth Gibb was perhaps a bit of an alarmist.

In his service that was a very damaging epithet indeed.

He read his original report again. Then, very deliberately, he tore it in pieces.

Francis Mason walked back to Parker's, turning up his collar against the bitter February. A crumpled newspaper blew past him on the sour grey wind, and for a moment he saw Seven bland in the summer sun. He shivered involuntarily. It was summer at Seven. The heat was on Seven in two senses, and in one of them it had followed him to London. But not the right one. He longed for the sun. He looked at the naked trees tossing uneasily against a liverish sky, and the generations of Candoran Masons stirred within him. They had said they were Candorans, and Francis at least meant it. It would be pleasant to be warm again. At Seven . . .

He was surprised how Seven had faded. London froze him with a crippling cold, but somehow it wasn't alien.

He walked into the excellent central heating of Parker's Hotel. It wasn't the same thing, but at least you could move in it.

Lavinia Mason was waiting for him in her bedroom. It was nearly lunch-time, but she hadn't yet dressed. There was a bottle of gin on the table beside her and a row of tonic waters. Francis noticed the crumpled tin-foil – the bottle was a new one; he noticed too that a third had been despatched. But his expression did not change. He knew that his wife drank more than was good for her – not sluttishly yet, simply more than was wise – but he had never commented. And not from fear. Rows he avoided, but he would have accepted one on a matter of principle. As, if she had loved him, her drinking would have been. As it was. . . . Well, he had married her; he knew she was unhappy. A little more gin than was discreet . . . He shrugged imperceptibly.

She greeted him, and he sensed at once an unusual nervousness. 'I want to talk to you,' she said. 'Sit down. Have a drink.'

Francis poured gin and tonic, sitting down on the chair of the dressing-table, waiting.

'I must talk to you,' she said again.

'All right.' It sounded more formal than he had intended.

'It's very difficult to start.'

'Start where you like,' he said smiling.

'Then I know why we're here, of course.'

'Of course you do.'

'But I want to know what's happening.'

'Nothing much yet. I went to the embassy this morning and saw a man called Menderez. I liked him, but we didn't reach terms.'

'Why not?'

'It's early days,' he said mildly.

'It's absurd.' Lavinia Mason did not hide that she was irritated.

Francis sighed. He was remembering that diplomats were supposed to be a race apart. It flattered them to think so and perhaps they were right after all. It was the easy explanation – Menderez could be putting on an act.

He was secretly sure he wasn't. There was something with Menderez . . .

His wife broke his train of thought. 'So what happens now?'

'They've asked us to a party this evening.'

'At the embassy?' For a moment she brightened.

'Yes.'

'That will be a change,' she said. Her moment of animation left her and she poured another gin. Presently she began again: 'Francis . . .' Her voice tailed away.

'Yes?'

'How much money have we? Here, I mean, in England.'

'What Granclegg smuggled out.'

'But how *much*?'

'Do you really need to know?'

She flared at him at once. 'Don't you trust me?'

'It isn't a question of trust. It isn't my money.'

'Granclegg,' she said contemptuously.

'He's secretive, I know, and arbitrary. But if he didn't tell you – '

'I never asked him,' she said. She spoke rather quickly.

'Well . . . '

'Damn it, I'm your wife. I've a *right* to know.'

'If you put it like that,' he said miserably.

'I most certainly do.'

'Fifty thousand,' he said. 'What he would have left my father, and perhaps a little for me. Three generations. Granclegg . . .'

'To the devil with Granclegg. He's a wicked old man.'

'He can certainly be difficult. One has to take him.'

'I can't. I *won't*.'

'I've always been sorry you didn't get on.'

'Get on,' she said, contemptuous again. 'Get on! I hate him. I hate Seven.'

'I know,' Francis said dully. 'I'm sorry.'

She sat still for some time, thinking intently. Francis watched her, empty of emotion. Once he had desired her. Now – now she wasn't a bad-looking woman. Gin hadn't yet blurred her figure, and in the suns of Seven she had taken good care of her skin. She looked severe, he thought, and he knew she was without compassion. A brittle woman, but an unhappy one. He was resentful and with reason, but he couldn't hate her. Nor could he guess what she was thinking – they had never been close enough, even at first. Nevertheless when she spoke she surprised him. 'That money of Granclegg's,' she said. 'Forget it. I've plenty of my own.'

'I couldn't possibly use your money on Seven. You must know that.'

'I didn't intend you to.'

'Then I don't understand.'

'You should do. I've some money, and when mother dies there'll be more. Enough, I should say.'

'Enough for what?'

She looked at him impatiently, uncertain whether he didn't understand or wouldn't. 'Enough to start again. In England. I could set you up.'

He was silent in turn. If she had expected surprise, a string of difficulties, he disappointed her. What at last he said was succinct, his voice entirely neutral. 'I've obligations, I'm afraid.'

It wasn't quite what she had expected, but she tried again.

'To whom?' she asked. 'To Seven?'

'No. Seven is Seven – I won't give it up unless I have to. But it wouldn't be true to say that I owe it an obligation.'

'To Granclegg, then?'

'Yes. While he lives.'

'I wish he were dead,' she said.

He looked at her again, but she had dropped her eyes. Not meeting his own she said slowly: 'Francis, I mean to stay here. I can't face Seven again.'

'I couldn't oblige you to.'

'Stay here too then.'

'You must see I can't do that.'

She began to cry, and Francis watched her. She had given him experience of false tears, but these could be genuine. He was sorry for her, pitiful, and he gave her the benefit of the doubt. On principle.

She looked at him at last, and now there was no doubt. She

was desperate. 'I'll do anything,' she said. 'Anything. You understand?'

He turned away, hiding his face till he had mastered it. God! she must be stricken. He knew she detested him, holding him to blame. And even if she meant it . . .

He didn't want her; he simply didn't trust her.

After a moment he said: 'I'm afraid it's too late.' He spoke quite politely, as though to a stranger.

She raised her head again, and what he saw frightened him. It was one thing to suspect, even, when you thought of it, to know, but to see that rigid mask, furious, hateful, and hating . . . 'All right,' she said. 'I gave you the chance. I thought I owed you that. And you throw it in my face. All right then. Every man for himself. From today. If that's the way you want it.'

CHAPTER SIX

THE Candoran embassy in Belgrave Square was a good deal larger than Candoro justified, and if the régime of the Romeros had been one where protest was judicious a good many tax-payers would probably have protested. But Candoro had been caught in the rat race of minor states living diplomatically beyond their means, and at the Court of St James in particular it was thought necessary that its representative should make a show. This the third of Romero's brothers was more than willing to do.

It was a splendid house for a party, and whatever his numerous vices Dickie Romero wasn't mean. His instincts were simple: he would have liked to get tight with his guests. Since his guests seemed to have absurd inhibitions on the matter, he simply got tight. At about half past seven the archivist took him away. He went perfectly quietly, for this was something he was used to.

The invitation had been for six o'clock, but Lavinia Mason had insisted that they shouldn't arrive before half past. In this she had shown wisdom, for at half past six they were almost the first arrivals. They accepted champagne, for His Excellency had a thing about gin. A peon's tipple, he thought it – *gaucho* and there-fore to be despised. He liked to consider himself civilized, and in more ways than one he had been successful. The embassy's salon was admirably decorated. It blazed with light but didn't wholly escape the slightly ecclesiastical gloom common to the reception-rooms of embassies. Perhaps it was the pictures, minor Spanish masters borrowed from the museum in Candoro's capital. They were intense and sometimes visceral. Nevertheless the effect as a whole was gay, a sort of come-and-get-it hospitality which wasn't common to the reception-rooms of embassies at all. By seven o'clock it was a party.

Francis Mason stayed close to Lavinia. Candoran acquain-tances greeted them, speaking Spanish and English equally. He watched her without appearing to. She loved a party, he was thinking, and she was good at them. For parties Lavinia Mason woke up. A less charitable man might have noticed that her gaiety was faintly febrile: all Francis noticed was that she was happy.

She smiled and she chatted and she joked; she was being a success and she was conscious of it.

Kenneth Gibb came up to them and, after a decent interval, Francis slipped away. In a corner Menderez was standing for a moment alone. Francis joined him. Menderez filled his glass from a bottle on the table behind him – it was that sort of party – waving his own at the roaring crowd. He was smiling sardonically. 'What a people,' he said in Spanish.

'It's a lovely party,' Francis said politely.

'Of course it is. Eats from your own kitchen and unlimited booze – of course it's a good party. I didn't mean that.'

Francis was silent, not knowing an answer, but Menderez went on. 'Mother of God! Look at them.'

Francis looked at them.

'You know what they're thinking?'

'No.'

'They're thinking of themselves – their careers, their urinal careers. The ones half-way up are thinking how to get to the top, and those near the top are wondering what sort of top. Will it be a plum – Rome, perhaps, or even Paris? Or will it be Bogotá and afterwards a hunt for second-rate directorships?'

'I can see it's a curious world.'

'It stinks,' Menderez said coolly.

Francis Mason laughed, and Menderez drank again. 'If you weren't a gentleman you'd be asking why I stayed in it.'

'I confess I'd wondered.'

'I'll tell you. There's so much to watch. I'm observant and I enjoy observing.'

'For instance?' Francis asked.

Menderez looked at him, evidently weighing a decision. At last he said: 'I don't know you very well. ....'

'Don't let that stop you.'

Menderez bowed. In a Spanish much more formal than they had been using he said: 'For example I am observing Mrs Mason. I am observing that she is talking, and with a notable animation, to a Señor Gibb. Whom I am inclined to mistrust. And I am observing Miss Kendrick. It is evident that she would enjoy your company, but it is a fact that you have not spoken to her.' Menderez broke off suddenly. 'Now you may strike me,' he said. 'It would be perfectly in order.'

'But a little out of date.' Francis discovered that he wasn't offended. Menderez was outrageous but he couldn't be disliked. A little surprised, Francis realized that he was liking him very much.

Menderez said slowly: 'One does not take such a risk in idleness. . . . Nor offend an acquaintance by suggesting a friendship.' But he raised his glass at Francis, drinking formally. Nothing was said. He put his glass on a table, and his casual manner returned. 'Well, I must get to work again. God knows what for.'

He bowed again and walked away.

Francis worked his way across the room towards Clare Kendrick, thinking that if Menderez could notice so could others. To ignore her wasn't safety, and it was also rude. She broke off a conversation at once. 'Hullo Francis.'

'Hullo Clare.' He was conscious he wasn't shining. 'Lovely party.'

'Glad you're enjoying it.'

Clare's escort of the moment coughed. 'Mr Mason,' Clare said, 'Captain Jay.'

'Delighted,' Jay said. It was obvious that he wasn't. He returned to Clare. 'You were saying . . . ?'

'Oh, I've forgotten.'

Jay looked at Francis Mason. 'Beastly cold,' he said.

'Horrible.'

'I gather you're from Candoro.'

'How?' Francis asked. He was smiling.

'Well . . .' Truth, if it had been possible, would have compelled Captain Jay to confess that Francis, wearing a suit excellent but ten years old, didn't look quite English.

But Francis rescued him. 'Yes, I'm Candoran.'

'You speak wonderful English.'

'We speak it at home, you know. When we remember to. And I was at school here.'

'Really?' Jay asked where, and Francis told him.

'Ah,' Jay said. He had been elsewhere.

'Jeremy,' Clare said, 'shut up.'

'Oh, sorry.' But he was a determined young man; he stood his ground.

Clare sighed softly.

'I'll come back later,' Francis said.

Jeremy Jay made a noise in his throat. In society less polite he would simply have said, 'Don't.'

Clare Kendrick said quietly: 'Please do.'

Francis Mason wandered away.

Menderez cut Gibb out with the skill of a sheepdog. Kenneth Gibb wasn't pleased, for he had been talking to Lavinia in a group which he considered both intelligent and useful to him. But he was obliged to admire expertise. There had been nothing crude, no nudging, no pulling of sleeves. One moment he had been talking in a group, the next he was alone with Menderez.

'Could we have a word?'

'Here?' Gibb asked. His manner was as formal as he could make it; he liked to think it quietly formidable. He wouldn't have admitted that he was feeling resentful towards Menderez, conscious of a tiny secret wound; he would simply have said that he didn't wish to be seen talking too earnestly in public. It was against the rules – unwise. 'Here?' he repeated.

'Come to my office if you like.'

'But we couldn't do that.' Kenneth Gibb spoke without affectation, for the suggestion horrified him. To leave a party openly with Menderez, your host ... In twenty-four hours it would be all over London, or all of it that mattered to him. 'Impossible,' he said shortly. He was genuinely annoyed.

'But why?'

'Damn it, you're a host.'

Menderez laughed. 'Precisely. So nobody is going to think you rude enough to carry me away. Ergo, *I* must have carried *you*. That's a black, perhaps – not in the book. But nobody will blame you. What you'll get is sympathy.' He waved a hand. 'It's that barbarian Menderez ...'

'I don't think we ought to do it.'

'Meaning you won't?' Menderez asked.

Kenneth Gibb was hating him. He hated a false position, and the man who put him there was hateful. 'You're making it very difficult,' he said. Now his voice was resentful.

'All right. Shall I come to the Foreign Office?'

'I don't know what we have to discuss. Not now, I mean, not after – '

'That's what I wanted to tell you.'

'Next week,' Gibb said vaguely.

'Of course. It's Saturday.'

'Next week, then.'

'Monday, perhaps?'

'I – ' Gibb began.

'I'm glad it suits you. Monday at eleven ... Will you have a drink?'

'No, thank you,' Gibb said.

By the time Francis Mason had wormed his way back to his wife, Gibb, too, had rejoined her group. Francis could see that she was in very good form. Not dangerously – she wasn't within distance of being drunk – but wine she had taken to her profit. He inspected her shrewdly and with experience, not seeming to. Five, she had had, he decided, and from five glasses of champagne she had borrowed a genuine sparkle. But with one or two more ... 'Were you thinking of dinner?' he asked her.

'I was not.'

'I was getting a bit hungry.'

'Try the eats if you're starving. They're excellent.'

Some idiot said: 'No, don't go.'

'I don't intend to.' She held out an empty glass. There was a bottle behind Kenneth Gibb, but he did not reach for it. 'Kenneth,' she said sharply.

'I'm sorry.' He filled the glass slowly, pausing as it was half-full. Lavinia Mason, saying nothing, held it, watching the wine increase. Gibb lowered the bottle at last and Lavinia raised her glass. She drank it deliberately, staring at her husband. 'Now ...'

'Now I think we'll go.'

'You can go. I'm going to dinner.' She laid her free hand on Kenneth Gibb's elbow. Her rings were magnificent. 'Kenneth,' she said, 'take me to dinner.'

He looked at her husband, but Francis was silent.

'Kenneth,' she said again.

'I ...'

She held out her other hand, the empty glass in it. 'Then give me a drink. Dinner or another drink.'

... Blackmail, he thought wretchedly, the bite again. It isn't my night.

57

With an evident reluctance he addressed Francis Mason. 'You don't mind?' he asked him.

'By all means.'

Lavinia Mason put her glass down. She took Gibb's arm and she turned to her husband. Now she was without pretence: her voice cut icily. 'Every man for himself,' she said. 'Don't say I' didn't warn you.'

The little group stood in an unhappy silence as she walked from the room with Kenneth Gibb She was still quite steady, and they were wishing she were not. That they could have excused.

Francis crossed at once to Clare Kendrick. He bowed to Jeremy Jay, but he didn't hesitate to interrupt him. 'Clare,' he said simply, 'will you have dinner with me?'

'I'd love to.'

'But,' Jay began, 'you said – '

'He's a visitor,' Clare said. 'I hardly ever see him.'

'But – '

'Luncheon tomorrow, then.'

'Tomorrow's Sunday.'

'Don't you eat lunch on Sunday?'

To his credit he laughed. 'All right. Say the Savoy.'

'Much too grand,' she said.

'Then make it Soho.'

'What's open on Sundays?'

He told her.

'Thank you very much. At one?'

'At one.' He turned to Francis Mason. 'And damn your eyes,' he said pleasantly.

At the door the vague counsellor was standing very upright. For a reason which people guessed, but wrongly, he was a tee-totaller. Very grave, quite deaf, he wished them good night. Menderez was standing by him. He wasn't less polite, but he was much less severe; he didn't look at Clare, but he shook Francis's hand. 'Good night,' he said. 'I wish I knew what money you had.'

Francis laughed. 'As I told you, that's the last thing on earth . . .'

'I'll have to find out, though. Good night again.'

Gog and Magog had stayed at the Office late that evening. It was something which neither did often, nor did they take work home: as a result, though both were in their fifties – Gog well on in them – both were in excellent physical shape. They did their jobs superbly but neither let it ride him. They were admirable public servants but they weren't slaves. They had seen too much of that sort of thing, and they were men of a cool wisdom.

Which they were now applying. The problem before them was Kenneth Gibb's report on Candoro – the amended report which he had finally sent up. It hadn't gone directly either to Gog or Magog, but the very senior official who had received it had shown it to them at once.

For he knew that Sir Godfrey Henn and Mr William Lampe-Lister were considering Kenneth Gibb for an important appointment, and he had thought this report very relevant to their decision.

He hadn't in fact much liked it, and Gog and Magog were liking it less. Sir Godfrey Henn was shaking his untidy head. 'I don't understand it,' he was saying. 'Anyone would think he had never been in Candoro; anyone would think he read nothing but the ambassador's dispatches.'

'Charles Withers is an ass.'

'Of course he is – that's why he's in Candoro. He's senior, well-connected, and a half-wit. There aren't very many of them left – we've practically sweated them out by now – but what there are we send to Candoro. Gibb will know that as well as we do. My point is that he sees plenty which Withers doesn't. You know where it comes from.'

'Certainly I do. We wouldn't dare show it to Withers even if we wanted to.'

'Yet Gibb comes up with this.' Gog tapped the report. 'I've been looking at his last two, and if I had to summarize them, I should use a phrase which he himself did.' Gog flicked the papers. '"Increasing tension",' he said.

'But now he's as bland as an Anglican bishop talking about doctrine.'

'And just about as definite.' Gog lit a cigarette from the inescapable crumpled packet. 'Why?' he asked.

'It isn't good to be wrong,' Lampe-Lister said slowly.

'But he's been there himself. He sees the stuff – the real stuff. And he hasn't been stupidly reassuring over the last few reports.'

'Admittedly.'

Sir Godfrey Henn struck the table. 'Then why the balancing act? Why this funambulist drivel?'

'It isn't wise to be wrong,' Lampe-Lister repeated. 'Not – not when you're in the running for an important job.'

Gog smoked deliberately for some time. At last he said: 'You're saying something serious.'

'I know it.'

'I wish I'd a better explanation – to knock down your own.'

'But you haven't?'

Sir Godfrey shook his head.

There was a considerable silence before he spoke again; he seemed to be quoting. 'He *has* something,' he said.

'And something he hasn't.'

Sir Godfrey Henn chuckled. 'We've had this conversation before.' He ground his cigarette out. '"Something he hasn't",' he repeated. 'May I – may I now ask what?'

'Integrity,' Magog said. He wasn't smiling.

There was another long silence which Gog broke with a sort of groan. 'We'll have to speak to him – it's only fair.'

'Of course.'

'I'll toss you who does it.'

'You damned well won't. You're the senior.'

'Oh, all right.'

Sir Godfrey lit another cigarette. 'And what will we use for NATO?' he inquired.

Magog sighed. 'We shall do a complicated shuffle and try and prise out Elliston from Moscow. Maston will kick like a mule, for he's only just gone there, and moreover it will all take time.'

'I'll have to talk to Gibb in any case. I needn't say anything about the NATO job. But he'll probably guess he's lost it.'

'I wouldn't be too sure.'

Gog was surprised. 'But he's not without finesse,' he said.

'Nor an evident capacity for deceiving himself.'

'William, you simply don't like him. I know I've said that before.'

'That's why I'm glad this has happened.'

'I take your point,' Gog said shortly.

'And I accept your apology.' Magog was very smooth. He sighed again. 'A complicated reshuffle,' he repeated. 'Three or four careers interfered with – I don't care a damn about that – it's my job. But four or five families uprooted, unexpectedly transferred ... Houses to find again, the children's education ...' He made a sound which in other than an Assistant Secretary of State would simply have been a snort. 'God damn Master Gibb,' he said.

Menderez walked back across the park to his flat in Bayswater. He lived simply but, with an admirable Scots housekeeper, not without modest comfort. He let himself in and picked from the mat an unstamped envelope, holding it for a moment, frowning. The amateurishness annoyed him. He knew what would be inside – a letter from Candoro. It would have been brought over on some Candoran ship; sneaked ashore by a seaman; passed to a contact. The contact was a penniless refugee. He would put the letter in another envelope, sealing it meticulously, delivering it by hand. It wasn't inconceivable that he had disguised himself. Or tried to.

Menderez's friends were that sort of people. He knew it, for he had no delusions that they were effective. Virtues they had – a hatred of Romero and a love of liberty. They were the stuff of martyrs but not of successful revolutionaries. Not like his other contacts, those he was deceiving, those he intended – never too hopefully – to use. His smile was grim, for he had assessed his risks. By God, they weren't negligible! If those others even knew that he was receiving letters from Candoro, letters from what they contemptuously called the bourgeois opposition ...

For those others were anything but amateurs, and they were notoriously mistrustful. It was quite probable that they were checking on him. Even in London. After all, they were international. They could be watching his flat, and what they would have seen would be a down-at-heels expatriate slipping a letter in the box. Inevitably he would have looked suspicious, for he would have been trying quite desperately not to.

And he could simply have posted it. That, though, was typical: he wouldn't have thought of anything so sensible.

Menderez sighed. He went into his sitting-room, opening his letter, reading it carefully. It was from a professor in one of the two universities, and it smelt of the academy – sincere, high-minded, politically quite futile. But one thing it told him, though

61

he doubted if it had meant to: his contacts, his other contacts were becoming increasingly strong. Six months he had told Kenneth Gibb – six months before Romero fell.

It looked like an overestimate.

His lean face tautened in the lamplight. ... Less than six months. Money they must have, money to bribe, to fix, somehow to win control of the machine. It wouldn't be easy – not that particular machine, for there was a hard hard-core, passionate, convinced. Men of the new religion these, but the rest ...

The rest were Candorans.

His smile held pity but humour too. He was Candoran himself.

Money, he thought again – money for the few essential arms in the few, the all too few essential hands. A hundred thousand should do it and fifty might.

Francis Mason must have fifty thousand pounds. He must.

The young man was saying to Amadeus: 'A Candoran refugee, a man Romero kicked out. An expatriate. What do you think he was doing at Menderez's flat?'

Amadeus said briefly: 'Find out.'

CHAPTER SEVEN

KENNETH GIBB arrived at the Foreign Office at five to ten on
Monday morning, and at a quarter past Sir Godfrey Henn summoned him. He was back in his own room in twenty minutes, a
little shaky and a little sick. For he could recognize disapproval
however smoothly administered. And it *had* been smooth, he
reflected sourly; it had been really beautifully done. Gog had had
Gibb's quarterly report on the table before him, and he had begun
by seeming puzzled; he had shown no emotion, certainly no irritation – just, to begin with, a bland incredulity. ... Were these
Gibb's considered opinions? Yes? Then he must realize that there
was room for others. An official was entitled to his opinions but ...

Gog's manner had changed almost imperceptibly, but Gibb
had been aware of it. Might Gog ask a question? Thank you.
Then, though he didn't wish to seem tiresome, had Gibb in fact
read all the material? All of it? The secret stuff, for instance – what
didn't go outside the Office? Yes again? In that case he need only
say that he ventured to dissent from Gibb's conclusion. Sir
Godfrey cleared his throat. Courteous in controversy, he was
offering the other his turn.

Kenneth Gibb took it. Now, back in his room again, he was
wondering whether he wouldn't have been wiser to have kept
silence. He moved his shoulders irritably. No, it wouldn't have
helped him. He could have agreed, expressing polite regret, leaving quickly; and that would have made it more difficult for Sir
Godfrey, since it would have denied him further opening. But it
wouldn't have removed from his mind the impression which he
had later hinted. That was what mattered – Gog's private opinion
of Kenneth Gibb.

In any case Gibb hadn't kept silence; he had begun to justify,
to dot the Is and cross the Ts, filling the gaps in. He was conscious
that he hadn't done it badly; he flattered himself that he had
shown no anxiety; he had spoken slowly and coolly, and Gog had
heard him impassively. At the end Gog had said, very carefully:
'I recognize the arguments.'

'And you don't agree with them?'

'No. But I didn't ask you here to tell you that.'

There was a silence broken as Gog blew his nose uninhibitedly. He put his handkerchief away. 'Outside this office', he said, 'is a very strange world. No, I should say that outside is the world and that this office is a very strange one.' He paused before he added: 'The more senior we get the more we have to recognize it.' He put on 'senior' an exquisite sub-emphasis.

'I hope I don't live in an ivory tower.'

'No. ...' Sir Godfrey Henn stared levelly at Kenneth Gibb. 'I wish I could think it was that. That can be remedied.' He rose, unexpectedly but firmly: the interview was at an end. He tapped the report on the desk before him, bland again, smiling pleasantly. 'Well, thank you for the work you've put in on this, and for your opinion too. I can't agree with it, and for that matter neither does Meadows. You'll understand if I ask him to re-write it.'

Gog walked to the door and opened it. He had excellent manners with subordinates.

And, Gibb thought, back in his room again, a formidable perception. Gibb was too experienced wholly to deceive himself: he had made a mistake and it would be stupid not to recognize it. 'That can be remedied,' Gog had said. What had the old bastard meant by that? What could be remedied? Not the suspicion that Kenneth Gibb was simply out of touch – Gog had denied that he nursed it, and Gog, though maddeningly Delphic, was far too intelligent to be untruthful. Gibb's secretary brought tea, and he drank it with ten grains of aspirin from the locked drawer below the bookcase. He began to feel calmer. A formidable perception. ... But it was possible to overestimate Sir Godfrey Henn. Something had gone wrong – childish to deny it – but it was probably only 'judgement'. Judgement was a wonderful word in the Service: there was a mystique about it. It didn't mean being right – Good heavens, nothing as simple as that! – but only holding the opinions which, at a given time, were acceptable to given superiors. Which, after all, Gibb had known when he had changed his report.

And changed it wrongly. That had been bad luck – bad judgement. But it wasn't final. Kenneth Gibb sent his secretary for a second cup of tea; he drank it smoking a cigarette, almost himself again. He had made a mistake, and one most unfortunately timed. But it needn't be fatal, as it would have been to cry woe

when Gog and that idiot Meadows were not or did not wish to;
and as for any thought that it could seriously prejudice his chances
for that job with NATO ...

He shook his head, for now he had persuaded himself. They
were much too fair-minded for that. An official was entitled to his
opinions – Gog had said so himself.

In the unexpected excitements of the morning, his own essays in
reassuring himself, Kenneth Gibb had forgotten his appointment with Menderez, and when his secretary telephoned that he
had arrived Gibb's first instinct was somehow to put him off. But
that was impossible now. He cursed himself irritably, for he was in
no mood for Menderez. If he had thought of it twenty minutes
before when first he had returned from Gog, before Menderez
had left his embassy, he could have told him some tale with at
least the hope that it might be believed; but now Menderez had
arrived it was inconceivable to refuse him. 'Show him up,' he
said resignedly.

Menderez, polite but not excusing himself, came in. Gibb
gave him tea and a cigarette, waiting for him to begin, collecting
himself. He had discovered that he was disliking Menderez
intensely.

'I need your help,' Menderez began.

'I was afraid it might be that.'

'Afraid?' Menderez sounded surprised.

'Well ... I didn't want to disappoint you.'

'You won't,' Menderez said calmly.

'I'm not sure I understand you.' Kenneth Gibb had begun to
bristle.

'Naturally it's about Francis Mason.'

'I guessed it might be when you made the appointment on
Saturday. But I'm sorry I can't help you there. You're in touch
with him and he with you. You're on your own. There's nothing
more I can do.'

'There's a great deal more.'

'I'm afraid I don't see it.' Gibb was being patient, conscious
that he was behaving rather well. He had a special manner for
the unreasonable request, for members of the public who were
influential enough to have been sent to him direct but who didn't
seem to realize that an official had his own rules. He was thinking

that such people could be excused: they were an occupational hazard, and it would be unreasonable to be annoyed with them. But Menderez wasn't the public; he was a colleague, an insider.

It was intolerable.

'I'm afraid I don't see it,' he said again.

'You will when I tell you.'

Gibb shrugged. 'All right.' He had meant to sound tolerant, amiably avuncular; he realized that he had almost snapped.

'I want you to find out how much money Mason has. Then, when you've done so, to tell me.'

'Good God.'

Menderez smiled. 'If you're wondering why, you're entitled to an explanation. Which is that we're not interested in haggling. If once we were we certainly aren't now. For us it's all or nothing. That has been decided.'

'And you suppose, you dare to think I would cooperate?'

'No, I don't think. I know.'

Kenneth Gibb got up. His lips moved soundlessly, breath came to him with effort.

Menderez didn't rise. 'Sit down,' he said.

Very slowly Gibb did so. He spoke with what he was sure was dignity but was in fact a good deal less. 'It is an impertinence,' he said pompously.

'Choose your own word.'

'I have done so.'

'I know a shorter,' Menderez said. 'Two syllables shorter. And it begins with B. I'm not ashamed of it.'

'How dare you!'

'In my knowledge of yourself. In the knowledge that you won't stand fire.' Menderez was maddeningly matter-of-fact.

'I think you'd better go.'

'I mean to. But this isn't a game. I should be less than fair if I didn't remind you of the circumstances.' Menderez finished his cigarette, speaking again impersonally. 'Kenneth Gibb is in the running for that job with NATO; Kenneth Gibb very much wants it. But this Gibb is also the lover of a Mrs Lavinia Mason whose husband is, shall we say, an official friend of Kenneth Gibb's. A sort of client. So that if his superiors knew this, it is highly unlikely that Gibb would go to Paris. Or anywhere else very much.' Now Menderez rose. 'Very unlikely indeed,' he repeated. 'You see what I mean? But of course you do. I can give you a week. Good morning.'

He walked coolly from the room.

He walked back to the Candoran Embassy across St James's Park, stopping to stare at the weather-bitten birds ... He had been a little severe with Kenneth Gibb, but it didn't disturb his conscience. At least he hadn't lied to him, nor told him half the truth; he had simply concealed it. Menderez disliked a lie, for in his profession it was the mark of failure, and the half-truth, though all too professional, he privately despised. Nevertheless it was a half-truth he had been obliged to tell Clare Kendrick – Clare whom he had personal reason to treat scrupulously. Not that she could even guess it. They had ransacked the ambassador's room together, to discover, he had explained, what the Romeros would accept; and on the assumption that they stood to gain a penny piece, the explanation had been legitimate. But in fact they did not. He had hinted as much, but he hadn't been able to tell her his full intention. He would have liked to – an ally would have been welcome – but it wouldn't have been fair to force on her a decision she hadn't sought. Menderez sighed. Fifty thousand, he had guessed: that was the minimum. A hundred thousand was too much: twenty, knowing the Masons, probably too little. He began to feel happier. For fifty could do it, fifty thousand for his friends, his real ones, not those others. . . .

On the bridge across the lake a young man joined him at the railing. He was very well dressed in an over-casual fashion, his waved head bare. Menderez had lived in London for three years, and he placed him at once. He began to walk away, furious when the young man joined him. 'No thank you,' he said crisply. 'Nothing doing.'

The young man laughed. 'You mistake yourself,' he said. He spoke in excellent Spanish.

Menderez stopped dead.

'I think we'd better keep moving. Less noticeable, you know.' They fell into step.

'I should identify myself,' the young man said.

'If you please.'

The young man said something in Spanish again. It was evidently a quotation. 'Satisfied?' he inquired.

'Perfectly.'

'I don't have a name, of course.'

'I don't suppose you need one.'

'No. And yours I know.'

'Then what have you to tell me?'

'Nothing. I was sent to ask.'

'They walked a few paces in silence.

'A Candoran went to your flat the other evening, a Candoran we know about. We know his politics, and their ultimate futility. We do not fear him, but it is foolish to take risks.'

'So?'

'Quesada's a fool, but he's something in his stupid party.'

They were in the Mall now, still walking together. Menderez was thinking fast; he saw the trap at once. 'Quesada wasn't his name,' he said.

The young man nodded coolly. 'It was not,' he agreed. 'You know it, though?'

'I do.'

'You met him, then?'

'I did not.'

'Then how do you know his name?'

'You saw him leave a letter.'

The young man nodded again. 'Yes. That's what I was coming to. ... What sort of a letter?'

'A begging letter.'

'To you? Officially?'

'In a way.'

'But he's a political refugee – the Romeros kicked him out. It's the penalty for inefficient intrigue. Yet you say he came to the embassy?'

'On the contrary, I said he came to me. You say he's a fool, and I dare say you're right, but he isn't fool enough to suppose he could get past the doorman at the embassy. Or that we'd answer a letter from him.'

'Quite. But he came to you.'

'We started from that.'

'Then why did he visit you?'

'Because even officials may be human. If he'd got inside the embassy I should have had him thrown out. I wouldn't have dared do otherwise. But at my home ... Perhaps, he thought ...

68

After all, I'm a Candoran, a Candoran in an official position. That's my use to you, if I have one.'

The young man smiled. 'To *you*?' he asked softly.

'To us might sound presumptuous.'

'I can see you've lived in England.'

'Three years.'

'Yes. . . . Believe me that I wasn't trying to trap you, or not at that moment, and the other you saw. But to return to this man. You helped him?'

'I did.'

'How?'

Menderez said reluctantly: 'I sent him a fiver.' He could lie when he had to.

'It was foolish.'

'It was unnecessary.'

'It was foolish. And you've seen him since?'

'I've never met him.'

'Nor written again?'

'No.'

The young man considered for a hundred yards of walking; then he said carefully: 'It sounds all right. I've have to report, of course, but I dare say we shan't meet again.' For a moment he hesitated. 'Will you accept advice?' he asked.

'Naturally. If it's good.'

'It's very good.'

'All right.'

'Watch it,' the young man said. 'I should watch it if I were you.'

That evening Kenneth Gibb took Lavinia Mason to dinner. He took her to a restaurant which he couldn't afford, for he had never learnt the art of hospitality. He would have been horrified to be told it, but he swung between the slightly mean and the unnecessarily extravagant. Taking a colleague to lunch, they would go to Gibb's club. Where he would offer the six-shilling, help-yourself luncheon. For six shillings it was London's best value, but it was scarcely distinguished. Unless, of course, the colleague were especially important, when Gibb would take him to Bloch's. As tonight he was escorting Lavinia. Bloch's was expensive. It had excellent service, a good deal of chi-chi, and rather poor food.

But it was undeniably fashionable. A woman more sensitive would have been embarrassed to be taken there by a man who she knew was neither on an expense account nor personally well-to-do, but Lavinia didn't consider it.

Gibb ordered champagne. He didn't consult Lavinia, for he had excellent reason to know that she wouldn't refuse it. Besides, champagne was champagne, a symbol. He didn't ask himself of what. There was a good deal of fuss with the sommelier, more with the head waiter. In the end they ordered borsch, a duck, *bombe surprise*, Scotch woodcock. It was rather a nasty meal.

Lavinia's conversation had surprised him. He had known that she wasn't considering marrying him: there were reasons, a dozen of them, not the least Francis. Francis Mason was old-fashioned, perfectly capable of sticking his toes in about offering evidence of misconduct he hadn't committed. So that Gibb hadn't expected talk of marriage, but nor had he expected that she would catalogue the stumbling blocks. Like most men Kenneth Gibb had assumed that a mistress would think as he did. He was spared the disillusion that she did not, but not astonishment that she should choose to recite their difficulties. They had never spoken of them. There were some things better unsaid.

That was very convenient, too.

'I can't think how you stand it,' she began.

'Stand what?'

'Your life. Your job.'

'It's not so bad. One sees the world.'

'One bums around it.'

'Not too uncomfortably.'

'Hired apartments and furnished houses. Ghastly parties on the *frais*. The same old faces.'

'You make a few friends.'

'What friends?'

He said a little stiffly: 'I'm sorry you don't like them.'

'I didn't say that.'

He managed a smile. 'Then what do you mean?'

'Only that *I* couldn't take it.'

'There are pretty good posts, you know.'

'Rome, Paris, Rio perhaps. Washington is hell.'

'I'll admit there are stinkers.'

'Like Candoro?'

He contrived to laugh convincingly. 'Candoro had compensations.'

'For you?'

'I'd hoped for you too.'

'Yes.' She drank some champagne. 'But I'm not going to be a diplomat's wife, so really it doesn't matter. What I don't understand is diplomats.'

'Why not?'

'Well, what do you really *do*? Where do you stand with other men?'

'Some of them envy us.'

'Yes. The wets, the arty ones, the social climbers.'

'You're not very kind tonight.'

'I'm never kind – I can't afford to be. At least I'm honest.'

'And bitter,' he said.

'Perhaps.'

He filled her glass again. 'I'm not sure what you're getting at.'

'I told you. I'm a woman. I might have been a diplomat's wife, but now I won't be. But if I were a man ...'

'Yes?'

'I should want a man's job. I should need it.'

He flushed. 'That's pretty bloody,' he said slowly.

'I'm not trying to hurt you.' But she spoke on coolly, not caring to smooth him. 'But what do you do – really *do*? What do you produce?'

'You approve of production?' he asked. He was trying to speak lightly.

'Don't slip me, Kenneth – swap punches. I don't worship production – I'm not American. I just admire producers.'

'Jalopies?' he asked her. 'Mozart's music?'

'Both.'

'Equally?'

'It's not for me to say. But for the men who make them – yes. Yes and yes and yes.'

'And I produce nothing?' He sounded defensive, though he hadn't meant to.

'Paper,' she said. 'Goodwill, if you're lucky. Sometimes. At huge expense.'

The waiter brought the extravagant ice-cream, and Gibb ate

71

his carefully. He was conscious that he must soon see his dentist. Trying to change the subject, and not too obviously, he asked her: 'What would you do if you were a man?'

'Work,' she said simply.

'But that's too easy. Work at what?'

'If I were a man I'd know.'

On an impulse he didn't analyse; not thinking, he said suddenly: 'You mean you'd compete.'

She put down her spoon, staring at him levelly, saying very quietly: 'Kenneth, you're not quite a fool.'

But he didn't want to pursue it. Instead he smiled. 'I'm glad.'

'Oh God,' she said. 'Dear God.' She sighed profoundly, finishing her wine. 'Kenneth, you're a falsie, half a man. . . . I'd like some brandy, please.'

Later he settled his considerable bill and the doorman found them a taxi. In it she took his hand. 'I was pretty bloody tonight.'

He began to feel better at once; he began to feel secure and generous. 'Forget it.'

'I have,' she said surprisingly. 'We'll go to your flat.'

He was terrified. 'We can't do that.' They had always been very discreet.

'We can and will. Francis is in the country.'

'I didn't know that.'

'Of course you didn't – I didn't tell you. It was all quite sudden.'

'But –' he began.

'He won't be back till midnight.'

'We could be seen, you know.'

'By whom? You live alone, don't you?'

'Well . . .'

'What a gambler you are!'

'I'm thinking of you,' he said stubbornly.

'Nonsense.'

There was a silence as the ancient taxi grumbled along Piccadilly. 'Infirm of purpose,' Lavinia said suddenly, 'give *me* the dagger.' She tapped on the taxi's glass partition, and the driver turned his head; he slid the panel aside. 'Madame?' he asked. He was quite an old man.

She gave him the new address.

Francis Mason had indeed gone to the country – if, he thought contemptuously, you called Blendon the country. It was a village near Guildford, and it wasn't a village at all. There were half a dozen farms, but they weren't being worked by men whose fathers had been farmers. There was a church, amalgamated with a parish a mile or so away. The vicar was a ritualistic young man with a voice a tone or two too high for undoubted masculinity. Besides, he was a bachelor. He wasn't very popular. There were shops and a Village Institute which the residents discreetly subsidized. Subsidy was the *leitmotif* of Blendon's life. It wasn't a community at all; or rather, what was left of the original lived without overt shame on the commuters who had absorbed it. It wasn't, recognizably, a village; it was a suburb with the props and fancies of the rustic meticulously preserved.

It was a curious place to have interested old Clegg Mason, but in fact its attraction had been simple: it was about the nearest to London he could keep a horse and find anywhere decent to ride it. Clegg Mason had taken a house there when last he was in England. That had been for his son's wedding. He had cantered across the Surrey heaths, upright, riding very long, a little absurd and more than a little splendid.

And now he had written to Francis in England he had wanted to know what was happening. Francis hadn't been greatly perturbed. It was inconceivable that Granclegg could leave Seven again: he must know that the journey would kill him. Not that that would stop him if he thought it essential. Which apparently he didn't, or at any rate not yet. He had inquired what progress had been made, inquired in his firm, still-beautiful handwriting. He had been a trifle testy but not, Francis decided, knowing him – not anything within distance of a genuine impatience. The nearest he had come to it was the remark that if things were going on like this much longer, then Francis had better see about that house in Blendon again. He, Clegg Mason, wasn't going to be mewed up in London. Not even to save Seven.

Francis hadn't taken him seriously: it was Granclegg's little pleasantry. But that February morning London had seemed intolerable. The twice-used air oppressed him, and he remembered Blendon. It was a travesty of what he considered country, but at least you could breathe there. He would have admitted that he was making an excuse to himself, but he had looked up the

73

trains to Guildford. I'll make a day of it, he thought; walk a bit; have supper there. In London his affair was at a standstill.

He told his wife he would be back about midnight. For once she hadn't objected. 'I'm dining with Kenneth Gibb,' she had said. 'That quite suits me.'

'And a theatre, I expect.' Francis hadn't been prying; he was indifferent whether they went to a theatre; he was making conversation.

'No, not tonight. I've letters to write. I'm a fortnight behindhand and I *must* catch up.'

'Don't stay up all night at it.'

'I won't. I'll be in bed before you're back.'

He had taken a taxi to the indeterminate fringe of Guildford, walking the rest in the bleak afternoon. He remembered the house and found it easily. He thought it appalling. It had belonged to a Trade Union official who, though he hadn't disgraced himself by making money, had undeniably married it. They had settled for a cottage expanded with great care by an architect not chosen locally. Inside it was very comfortable, but outside they had had to be discreet. In its sly way the house was twice as big as it looked. They had built a second garage for the other car, but not before they had grown a hedge, a high hedge of macrocarpa to screen it from the road.

The Trade Union official was dead, but his widow remembered Clegg Mason. . . . So this was his son? The house had been taken for his marriage, hadn't it? It seemed longer ago than that. Well, she wasn't exactly *trying* to let, but of course for old friends . . . If Francis could let her know more exactly . . .

She rambled on and he escaped at last. He walked again, then, looking at his watch, slipped into what was called the local. It was less like a local than anything he could remember – chromed and slick, with a white-coated barman. It was owned by a London syndicate which bought up inns in the Martini belt of upper suburbia and bastardized them. At the bar were two blondes – Surrey blondes, Francis thought elliptically, the sort you could only see in better night-clubs and this particular brand of pub. And with them George Gilson.

He hailed Francis at once, and Francis, barely remembering him, went over to them. He had known George Gilson at

74

school, and he hadn't much cared for him. One of the blondes belonged to him; the other – obviously this was great good fortune – the other would do for Francis. It was all very fortunate, extremely well-met. There were drinks and drinks again. And then more drinks. Afterwards there was a very bad dinner.

Francis longed for London.

Later, mentioning his return, he put his foot in it. George Gilson wouldn't hear of a train. It appeared he had a car outside, a fast and splendid car. He began to praise it. Besides, what about Mavis? Mavis was the other blonde. Francis couldn't do that to her.

He could have choked her cheerfully.

They climbed into the car, Francis and the second blonde behind. It was quite a good car but not quite safe as Gilson drove it. Francis was rather frightened: so was the blonde. She was also half-tight. She held his hand; then his arm; then, as Gilson showed off on the corners, slid into his lap. She did it very neatly, for it was something she had practised. She raised her painted face.

Francis obliged her, for he was a considerate man.

He left them at last at Parker's, promising engagements which he was determined to avoid. They had driven very fast and it was barely eleven. His head ached miserably. He searched his room for aspirin: apparently he had mislaid it. He walked to Lavinia's, knocking gently. He knocked again, then felt the handle. She hadn't locked the door. Well, he needn't wake her; he knew where she would keep it.

He went in very quietly.

The curtains were undrawn, and the glow of the street lamps lit the room softly. It was empty.

Francis Mason stood still for some time. He had forgotten about the aspirin. Then he went back to his own room.

. . . She had been explicit, he remembered – unusually emphatic. She was dining with Kenneth Gibb but she wasn't going on to a theatre. She had letters to write; she was behind-hand with her letters and she *must* catch up. But he wouldn't himself be back before midnight. . . .

He told himself it didn't mean a thing. She could have gone to a theatre after all; she could have changed her plans; she could

75

have gone to her mother's. She might ring from the country in the morning. It didn't mean a thing – not alone.

Francis Mason did not go to bed. Instead he took his overcoat again. He went for a grim, a solitary walk.

CHAPTER EIGHT

MR WILLIAM LAMPE-LISTER had made his arrangements much faster than he had given himself credit for. In any case, the blow wasn't the lighter that it came quite casually. Gibb had opened the envelope indifferently. It was marked STAFF and CONFIDENTIAL, but the latter meant little. Gibb had expected simply a staff circular, a record of retirements, deaths, minor postings. Major postings would be recorded too, but a counsellor didn't first hear that he had been transferred by reading a staff circular. Kenneth Gibb slit the envelope carelessly.

To be Counsellor at Paris, attached to the North Atlantic Treaty Organization and with local rank in Gradè V ... Mr P. L. Elliston, C.M.G.
To be Counsellor at Moscow in the vacancy of Mr P. L. Elliston ...

For a moment it didn't connect; for another he didn't believe it; then he thought he would be sick. He fought himself grimly, furious at the image which, uninvited, presented itself. It was that man at the Law Courts. Gibb had dropped in there with half an hour to kill. The prisoner had seemed quite calm – almost confident. He had had the air of a man with convictions but not too many. The jury had filed back slowly. Seven years, the judge had given him, seven years preventive. He hadn't believed it. 'Seven years,' he had kept on saying. 'Seven years.' Then he had collapsed.

In the end they had carried him away.

With a clean pocket handkerchief Kenneth Gibb wiped his face, then, with distaste, his hands. A thought had come to him and he despised it. For this couldn't be a hoax, an over-elaborate and ill-intentioned leg pull. That sort of thing didn't happen. Nevertheless he looked at the circular again, finding the name of a man he knew, a man posted from the Office on promotion. Hating himself, Gibb took the telephone.

'Peterson,' it said.

'Kenneth Gibb here. I see you're going to B.A.'

'But how kind of you to ring!' In a gentlemanly way Peterson was jubilant.

'Congratulations,' Gibb said slowly.

'Thanks. It'll be tough, of course – mountains of work. But the climate's not too bad.'

'Not too bad in winter.'

'And we can use the extra money,' Peterson said unexpectedly. 'Three boys and a bun in the oven. . . .'

'Congratulations again.'

'Well, I don't know. . . .'

'Anyway, good luck.'

'Thanks again. Good of you to ring.'

Kenneth Gibb put down the telephone, forcing himself to think. His bright little world was in ruins, but he wasn't without stamina. He still felt sick, and he was still sweating; he didn't remember lighting the cigarette which he discovered was burning his fingers. He looked at it with disapproval, for his hand was trembling. He put the cigarette out and, with an effort near physical pain, settled to think.

There could be only one explanation: Menderez had blown on him. He couldn't think why, there wasn't a motive. Menderez's interest was to keep him on the hook, to use him – blackmail him. He had admitted it in terms. It would be insane to destroy his own weapon. But there wasn't another explanation, not an acceptable one. It could only have been, *must* have been Menderez.

In a voice not quite steady Kenneth Gibb told his secretary to telephone to Señor Menderez. . . .

'Menderez? This is Kenneth Gibb. I wanted to see you.'

'But delighted. Where?'

'Can I come to the embassy?'

'Of course.'

'It's rather urgent, too.'

'Then come at once. I'll expect you in ten minutes.'

Gibb took a taxi to Belgrave Square and was taken immediately to Menderez. Fury had lent him something which was nearly dignity. In Menderez's room, not sitting down, he said almost crisply: 'What the devil are you at?'

Menderez looked astonished. 'I don't know what you mean.'

Gibb looked at him. If he's an actor, he decided, he's a good one.

'Won't you sit down?'

'I prefer to stand.'

Menderez shrugged. It had occurred to him that Kenneth

Gibb was drunk. It wasn't likely, but with the English you could never tell. These incredible officials . . . The bottle in the desk, the sudden irresistible temptation. And always when you least expected it. Menderez inspected Gibb thoughtfully. He did look very strained – wild, but in some odd way more human. If he were drunk Menderez preferred him so. 'I'm listening,' he said.

With an evident effort Gibb controlled himself. 'I've reason to suppose you've told my superiors about myself and Mrs Mason.' The sentence didn't strike him as particularly ponderous.

Menderez made a *moue*. This was Kenneth Gibb again, the normal one. Menderez was disappointed.

'Why on earth should I do that?'

'I came to ask you.'

'Well, I haven't.'

'You swear it?' Gibb heard himself saying.

'I swear to nothing. Our relations aren't relations of honour. But I ask you to think.'

'I have.'

'Then I can only say you've made a mess of it. I want something from you still; I'm making you give it me; but I haven't yet got it.'

Kenneth Gibb was silent.

'Damn it, use your head. You're making me guess what's really brought you here, but presumably somebody's discovered you're Lavinia Mason's lover.' Menderez leant forward. 'Are you sure of that?' he asked.

Very slowly, reluctantly, Kenneth Gibb shook his head.

'But something has happened?'

'It certainly has.'

'You'd better tell me.' Menderez was wholly collected; he waved at a chair. 'Sit down,' he said again.

Kenneth Gibb sat down. 'You'd better tell me,' Menderez repeated.

Gibb discovered that he could do so; he needed to tell somebody – even Menderez would do. 'I haven't got NATO,' he said.

There, it was out. He was disgraced.

Menderez didn't seem to think it disgraceful. Kenneth Gibb wasn't sensitive: if he had been he would have been offended at how calmly Menderez took it. 'Really?' he asked.

'I'm afraid not.'

'You'd take it as an insult if I commiserated. And rightly. So I won't. Instead I'll ask questions again.' Menderez smiled amiably. 'We ought to get this straight – for both our sakes.'

'It's straight enough to me,' Gibb said grimly.

'Indeed? Then you have the advantage of me. As I see it, you've learnt that you're not going to NATO. You at once conclude that somebody has sneaked on your private life.' Menderez cocked an eyebrow. 'Is that correct?'

'I suppose so.'

'So you thought it must be me?'

'I'm pretty sure nobody else knows. For that matter I don't know how you found it out yourself.'

Menderez waved this aside. 'We won't go into that. Nor the reasons, which in any case I've given you, why it was stupid to think I'd tell tales. Yet, that is. What puzzles me is something else.'

'What's that?'

Menderez didn't answer directly. 'You're not going to NATO,' he said again, 'and you thought the reason must be dirty work?'

'I suppose I did.'

'Odd,' Menderez said. 'People are very odd.'

'I beg your pardon?'

'Nothing. I was talking to myself. It's very rude and I apologize.' Menderez offered a cigarette and lit it. 'Nothing else struck you?'

'Nothing yet.'

'For instance it didn't occur to you that if you're not going to NATO you needn't fear Menderez? You didn't think that Menderez had nothing on you now?'

Kenneth Gibb sat silent again. It hadn't occurred to him, and he was kicking himself. He hadn't considered, he hadn't *thought*; he had acted on impulse; he hadn't done his home-work, and that was a crime. Very carefully he said: 'I can see it, of course.'

'I was afraid you might say that. If you're thinking like that I can only say – Don't. You're not going to NATO but you've plenty to lose still. Everything, in fact. You've nothing outside your pay, I think, or very little. You're too old for a middle-piece job in industry and not sufficiently senior to be offered a sinecure. You've got to stay in the Service, you know. If I let you.'

'Damn you,' Gibb said weakly. 'Damn your eyes.'

'As you please. I've a job to do.'

'It does you no good to destroy me.'

For a moment Menderez was irritated. 'Good?' he said shortly. 'That's quite irrelevant. I'm not a malicious man, and the word's out of context in any case. Sensible men aren't revengeful. Or', he added thoughtfully, 'not unless they have reason to be. That would be different. If it ever occurred.' He seemed to be talking to himself again. After a little he rose. 'I hope we understand each other. There isn't any change – not between you and me. I gave you a week, I believe. Today is Wednesday. That's two days gone.'

Kenneth Gibb took another taxi back to the Foreign Office and summoned his secretary; he told her that he wasn't feeling well – no, nothing to worry about, a chill possibly, but he was going home. He'd telephone if he still wasn't up to it tomorrow.

He took his third taxi of the morning, reflecting that it had been an expensive one.

In his flat he made himself think calmly. ... Menderez had been right; Menderez still had him. The Service was his life – a way of life. A splendid phrase, he thought sardonically, hallowed by generations of loose thinking. But the Service was also something else. It was bread and a little butter.

At thirty-nine it wasn't so easy to earn it. Not when you hadn't a trade. Just the same, if you did get a job outside ...

If you did find a job outside you could spit yourself of Menderez.

Kenneth Gibb began to consider Tom Ormonde. He had run into him again quite casually a fortnight before. Tom Ormonde was an industrial chemist, a director of an excellent family firm, and Tom Ormonde was in something of a spot. He was the third generation of chemist Ormondes: his drugs were a household name. He was prosperous – Kenneth Gibb thought him rich – but the Big Boys were after him. They spoke of an amalgamation; they were impeccably polite; but Tom Ormonde wasn't a fool. He knew that behind the politeness, the studied commercial courtesy, was what Gibb would have called a sanction – join us or we'll break you. Ormonde had explained that they could do it, too. Tom Ormonde had two new drugs coming on – winners he had thought – but he had spent a lot of money on them: his resources in ready cash were low. Probably the Big Boys knew it – in any case they'd timed it well. Six months of anything like serious price war and Ormonde's would be flat.

Kenneth Gibb had listened politely but without much interest. Other people's troubles ... He wasn't a chemist now, he was a diplomat. ... Or was he? He wouldn't stay one long if Menderez went after him.

He had taken Tom Ormonde's address and, later that evening, he rang his flat. Ormonde had seemed surprised, but he hadn't an engagement. 'Come round,' he had said. 'Tonight.'

Kenneth Gibb went round. He started very cagily, flattering himself that one thing the Service gave you was finesse. It would be a pity, he began, if a firm as old as Ormonde's went to the wall. And with good stuff coming along. He had been thinking about their conversation the other day, wondering. ...

Tom Ormonde had interrupted him. He was shrewd, trained in a hard school, and he was aware that he was being approached long before Gibb had intended it. Ormonde had been rather tickled. Diplomats, he reflected – they thought they were terribly subtle. He had listened until he was sufficiently amused; then he had interrupted. 'You're not a chemist now,' he had said.

'No.'

'You were damned good once – I grant you that. You could have gone places. I often wondered why you changed.'

'I was practically shanghaied, you know. They were terribly short of overseas staff. And after the war it didn't seem worth it to change again.'

'You're thinking of it now?'

'Perhaps.'

Tom Ormonde rubbed his chin. 'You'd have fifteen years to catch up on.'

'If I could get with people I knew, perhaps ...'

Ormonde said bluntly: 'It isn't chemists I'm looking for, how-ever good. I'm looking for money.'

'A lot of it, I imagine.'

'It depends what you call a lot.'

'Ten thousand pounds?'

Ormonde laughed. 'Nearer fifty.'

Gibb drew a deliberate breath. 'Fifty thousand to buy in?' he asked.

'Fifty thousand to buy in. A seat on the Board, of course. Three thousand a year and expenses, plus income on your share. Technical knowledge useful and acceptable, but it wouldn't be what we'd take you for.'

'Interesting,' Gibb had said.

He had left Ormondes in his fourth taxi of the day. He had gone there by bus, but a man hinting at five figures could hardly leave in one Tom Ormonde had telephoned to the rank, and in the taxi Kenneth Gibb had made up his mind. Ormondes was first class – he had known them for years, for they had been his own firm's competitors. Their barbiturates were as good as any, and they marketed competently.

Only one thing was wrong. He didn't have fifty thousand pounds; he hadn't ten; he hadn't in fact a penny. Fifty thousand pounds . . .

Well, he would have to get it.

That evening he took Lavinia to Bloch's again. He had looked at his bank account before he did so, frowning uneasily. But he took her to Bloch's. He had something quite special to ask of her.

He saw at once that she was in much better humour, and he thought he knew the reason. He wasn't a man with much experience of women – he thought of Lavinia as decidedly a feather in his cap – and his opinions of them were extravagantly over-simplified; they swung between the romantic and the grossly physiological. As a result he thought he knew why Lavinia was in better temper.

It didn't occur to him that he was still an adolescent.

Nevertheless it was a fact that she was in very good form. Kenneth Gibb scented success. He had considered the evening – its conversation and how he should handle it; he wouldn't again make the mistake he had made with Menderez, rushing in un-prepared, getting caught by the unexpected question. He had briefed himself very carefully, for he had realized that this even-ing could be vital to him.

He began from their conversation two evenings before. Smiling his most social smile he said: 'I gathered on Monday that you didn't think much of diplomats.'

'Oh, don't let's start that again.'

83

'Just as you like. But I've been thinking about it. I think you're right.'

'You do?' She was surprised and sounded it.

'Yes, in a way. It's really a closed circuit. You could make a machine which would be a perfectly good diplomatist, but the diplomatist couldn't make the machine.'

'Kenneth, you astonish me.'

'I don't see why, I'm not dyed-in-the-wool in the Service, you know. I was a chemist once.'

'A long time ago,' she said.

'Fifteen years. I hanker for it sometimes, though.'

'You do?'

'Yes.' He smiled again. 'And we were talking about competing. . . .'

'Don't you compete in the Service?'

'Of course we do. Polite faint praise to damn the other man, little barbed Minutes.'

'So I've heard,' she said dryly.

'And you mentioned production. We don't produce a thing. Not even a balance sheet.'

'Which isn't much good if it shows a loss.'

He looked at her, sensing a change in her manner. She was very good-looking, very desirable. Firm little chin, good skin still, very blue eyes. Her frock displayed elegant shoulders, her hair, still fair, was beautifully attended. An angel, he thought, an angel by a lesser Florentine. An angel who had spent a year at a worldly and very fashionable finishing school.

As indeed he knew she had.

He looked at her again, much less sure of himself. She looked like an angel but she would be a very tough one. Almost apologetically he said: 'I'd like to work again – really to work. You ought to understand that.'

'I didn't say I don't,' she said.

'Chemistry again for preference.'

'You're rather old to change.'

'Yes. . . . As it happens I know an opening.'

'A good one?'

'Have you heard of Ormondes?'

'Of course. Sleep in little tubes. I use a lot of it.'

'It's very good stuff.'

84

'You should know. It works with me, or mostly.'

'Ormondes might take me in,' he said. He was trying to sound casual.

'Really? At anything like your present pay?'

'Not on a salary at all.'

'They've asked you to join the Board?'

'More or less.'

'What's the less?'

'They want me to put up money.'

'Hm. ... How much?'

'Fifty thousand pounds.'

'I didn't think you had it.'

'I haven't.'

Lavinia Mason helped herself to champagne; she drank it slowly, and when she spoke it was with a tolerance wholly insulting. 'Kenneth,' she said, 'you're very simple, very young. You're asking me to stake you. Women do that sometimes – for husbands. A husband is something you have: husbands are *there*. That's important, you know, to a woman – being there. You're not my husband.'

He didn't try to answer her.

'If Francis were a different sort of man, more manageable ...' Her manner changed again as she leant forward. Her breasts were as firm as apples. 'Or you were,' she said deliberately.

'I don't know what you're getting at.'

It was a lie.

'No. That's what's wrong with you, Kenneth. You're intelligent, you're civilized. You're a man, but you're not. Anything violent, anything simply natural – it would never occur to you.'

'Damn it, it's the twentieth century.'

'Oh quite.' She seemed to have lost interest in the subject, eating for a while with appetite. He was thinking that he desired her; he desired her but he didn't much like her. Her question shattered him.

'Why do you want to leave the Service?'

'I told you; I want to go into business.'

'I don't believe you,' she said coolly.

'Why not?'

'Because you're not the man to. You love your Service, love your kennel. One day you'll be Sir Kenneth, and God, how you'll wag your tail! Not to put a point on it, I don't think you're telling the truth.'

He was silent again.

'Well?' She was smiling a smile he hadn't seen before. It was almost maternal. 'Well?'

A little sulkily he said: 'I may *have* to go.'

'*Have* to go? Axed? The promising Kenneth Gibb?'

'Not axed.'

'Sacked then?'

'It's possible,' he said miserably.

'But why?'

Reluctantly, stammering a little, he told her. The words came tumbling in spouts and gushes, unrehearsed. This hadn't been his plan at all. She listened in a long silence.

'How did Menderez find out?'

'I don't know that.'

'It doesn't matter. .... So he's blackmailing you?'

He nodded, not meeting her eyes.

'He wants to find out what Francis has? He wants the maximum?'

'He does, I'm afraid.'

'I'm in this too – my God I am!' She lit a cigarette. Smoking between courses wasn't one of her normal vices. 'I'll tell you,' she said finally.

'You can't,' he said. He hadn't meant to.

She looked at him with contempt. 'From you,' she said. 'That from you.' She leant forward again, decided, decidedly formidable. 'Do you think I'll be dragged through some squalid court? Do you think I'll be sniggered at at beastly parties? Or be rolled in a gossips' gutter?'

'There are more in this than you and me.'

'If you mean Francis, *I* will judge that. I owe little to Francis and nothing to Seven. I hate it. Francis won't starve for Menderez bleeding him. You're innocent, Kenneth – innocent but not innocent enough. Total innocence is shield and buckler. You haven't that. Come to think of it, you haven't anything.' She ground her cigarette out. 'Fifty thousand pounds,' she said.

Amadeus and the young man were talking again. 'I did what you told me,' the young man said.

'How?'

'I asked him directly what was the message that refugee left for him. He said it was a begging letter. Romero having kicked him out he wouldn't dare go to Romero's embassy. Instead he went to Menderez privately ... or so Menderez said.'

'And?'

'And he was lying,' the young man said. 'That's bad.'

'How do you know?'

The beautiful young man looked at his pointed shoes. 'I checked back on it. I picked up this refugee man in a café in Theobald's Road. It wasn't difficult, but he wasn't for me. So I got hold of Doris.'

'And Doris took him home?'

'Yes. Where she demanded several times what they'd agreed. Naturally he couldn't pay it.'

Amadeus said with distaste: 'No doubt there was the usual scene?'

'Not quite. She asked him if he was Spanish or South American and he said he was Candoran. Doris can be marvellously innocent, so then she asks him whether he couldn't raise it from Candoran friends. He said he didn't have any. "Not even at the embassy?" Doris says. He looks at her hard and laughs like crazy. "Not even at the embassy," he says. "Nobody there would give me a crust or ever has. They wouldn't dare."'

'Interesting,' Amadeus said. 'Very interesting indeed. You did well.'

'Thank you. And now?'

'Now I shall think.' Peter Amadeus lit a cigar and did so for ten minutes. At the end of them he said: 'So Menderez is suspect at least, and for suspects there is a standard ploy. You test them.'

'Quite. ... But how?'

'We will tell Señor Menderez that this money is important, though it isn't. We will tell him that it mustn't reach Candoro. Instead he's to get it and hand it to us.'

'Permission to speak?' the young man asked. He had done his National Service and had hated it.

Amadeus smiled. 'Go on.'

'Do you think that's enough?'

'I'm afraid I don't follow.'

'Suppose Menderez doesn't produce this money?'

'Then we'll listen to why not. If it sounds convincing, though I doubt it, if we're satisfied that nobody else has received it either, then I suppose we'd be much as we were. But if we find it's gone elsewhere, then Señor Menderez is for it.'

'Yes.' The young man stiffened. 'But suppose he *does* hand it over?'

'Well?'

'But is it so well? What would that *establish*? Only that we'd scared him into giving it us. It wouldn't prove the negative; it wouldn't show us his original intention.'

Peter Amadeus considered this. He was smiling as he said: 'You're a very suspicious man.'

'You trained me to be.'

'I seem to have succeeded.' Amadeus began to pace his too-carefully decorated room. 'Get hold of him,' he said finally. 'Tell him to get the money. Give him ten days. That's a sound enough plan as far as it goes. As for the rest, what are you proposing?'

'That we go to the source again – the source of suspicion.'

'This refugee?'

The young man nodded.

'And frighten the whole truth out of him?'

'Exactly.'

Amadeus smiled again. 'I don't think that's quite your line,' he said.

'I wasn't suggesting it. The decision will be yours, and so will the choice of men.'

Amadeus sat silently for some time. At last he said: 'I agree again. Send Lucca and Brutus Levy.'

'Lucca and Brutus, eh? That's quite a high horsepower.'

'If you're right it's quite a big motor-car. But tell them to be sensible. Go yourself too if necessary. I'm not convinced that this is worth trouble, or at any rate not yet. So there mustn't *be* trouble. Nobody in hospital, you understand – no nonsense with the police. Minimize it. If you're right, if Menderez has been playing us all the time, then something will have to be done about Master Menderez. And that will be more than minimal. So don't risk a minor heat just as we may have to start a major. Don't be extravagant.'

'I won't.'

'I know it. But try and get it through to those gorillas. If they smell blood and mess it up they're out on their own. They'll know what that means.'

'They'll know all right,' the young man said.

Francis and Clare Kendrick were at a cinema. He had been seeing a good deal of her, and with a conscience much clearer than he had expected. She was more than half-asleep. They had spent the afternoon at Richmond, riding in the park. Francis smiled. She had ridden in a black habit, side-saddle. Beautiful boots had peeped below her skirt. She had been wearing a stock and a hard hat; there had even been the suspicion of a veil. It had been an impertinence but a successful one. Beside the jodhpured rabble, men hatless, women in green huntsman's caps, she had looked ... well, she had been showing off perhaps, but certainly she had succeeded. A very old gentleman had actually clapped. Francis chuckled.

'What's the joke?'

'Nothing.'

'I was half-asleep. It isn't a funny film, is it? I'll wake up if it's a funny film.'

'It isn't a funny film.'

'I'm glad in a way. I'm terribly sleepy. All that fresh air ...'

'It's not one to wake up for.'

'I'm glad.'

He took her hand, and her arm went round his waist. The cinema was warm and dark, a thousand separate worlds. She sighed, a healthy animal healthily tired. She raised her lips and he took them.

She was very much nicer than the Surrey blonde.

CHAPTER NINE

KENNETH GIBB woke next morning with a sense of well-being. He lived in a flat in Campden Hill which he couldn't fully afford. There was a good sitting-room, tiny bedroom, bathroom, and kitchenette. The rent was severe and he had paid a considerable premium. But the address was right. He made his own breakfasts, and what he called his woman would, if he asked her, leave something in the evening which he could put into the oven. He didn't often ask her, preferring to eat out or not at all. Quite often it was the latter, for he had begun to watch his weight.

This morning he rose blithely, cooking his breakfast before he shaved, for he was unexpectedly hungry. The world was good; it could always be managed. Lavinia was mad, of course – quite crazy. Hinting at his killing Francis Mason! What did she think he was – an animal? The odd thing was that he had caught himself considering it. Naturally not seriously – he insisted on that. It had been purely an intellectual exercise, but he had found himself thinking about it as he read himself to sleep the night before. It had been a detective story, a poison case over-ingenious. Gibb couldn't help feeling that he could have managed it better. After all he was a chemist, and he was much too intelligent to be over-cunning. That was how poisoners always got caught – being too clever. He would use something simple, a household drug like one of Tom Ormonde's. None of them was poisonous, or at least not technically, but overdoses could be. Yes, that would be the technique: slip your man an overdose. You would have to plan it, and perhaps to wait on opportunity. And it might well look queer unless the victim was already an addict of the excellent Ormonde's excellent products. That was the point, though: you mustn't *mind* if it looked queer, mustn't try to make it otherwise. That was the way you tripped yourself. A coroner's jury, the police even – let them suspect if they wanted to. There was a gulf between suspicion, even a private certainty, and a case the police dared act on. Never try to close it. You only built a bridge, and the police walked over it. Straight to your front door.

Kenneth Gibb chuckled, staring at his image in the shaving glass. He was an intellectual with an intellectual's insatiable

curiosity in his own processes of thought. He had thought, how-
ever casually, of killing. His face looked just the same, though,
and it mildly surprised him. Not a bad face, he decided – the face
of a man who had considered a killing.

But that was rubbish, wholly a fantasy. He needn't kill a fly.
All he need do was call on Menderez.

He began to consider how he should do so, and when. He
remembered that he had been given a week, and that ran till
Monday. Menderez, damn him, had given him a week, and it
went against the grain to risk the impression that he was anxious.
Damn the man, he'd keep him waiting; he'd wait till Monday
and let him sweat a bit. Not that Menderez had seemed impatient; he had been odiously, insultingly collected; he had held
the cards and had shown that he knew it; he hadn't bothered to
pretend. Which of course was a breach of the rules. But that
was the trouble with Menderez – he was incalculable, you couldn't
rely on him. It wasn't inconceivable that he would change his
mind, and if he were to. . . .

Kenneth Gibb frowned. It was better to get it over. He'd
call on Menderez at once, before he himself went to the Foreign
Office, and without an appointment. That was something not
ordinarily done, something a little brusque and casual. Kenneth
Gibb would emphasize it; his manner would convey . . .

He smiled again. Face would be saved and that was important.
This would be a private compromise, and compromise, deep in
his blood in any case, was by now second nature.

He looked at his watch, deciding that he would walk to
Belgrave Square. He timed it to arrive at a quarter past ten, and
at twelve minutes past he was giving his name to the porter. He
wouldn't have been surprised to be kept waiting – not too long,
though – but Menderez himself came down to the waiting-room.
'So you're here,' he said calmly. 'We'd better go upstairs.'

Kenneth Gibb followed him. He had never before been in
Menderez's room, and immediately he disapproved of it. It was
furnished with fine pieces, but it was very untidy. Gibb began to
think what he would do with it: it could be made decidedly
impressive. Change the desk, of course – it was much too small.
Deeper pelmets, and loop the curtains. Throw away that reading-
lamp. No doubt it was efficient, but it was quite unsuitable for an
embassy.

'Well?' Menderez asked.

'I hope I'm not interrupting you. I'm afraid I hadn't time to telephone.' Kenneth Gibb was being calculatedly polite.

'Forget it.'

Gibb decided to forget it. Menderez watched him impassively. Presently he began to smile.

Kenneth Gibb hated him.

'You're not here for nothing,' Menderez said.

Gibb made another attempt at dignity. 'You asked me for certain information ...'

'Not certain information – that sounds like a policeman in a magistrate's court. I asked you how much money Francis Mason had.'

'If you prefer it.'

'I do prefer it.'

... Damn you, damn you, damn you.

'And I think you've come to tell me.'

'For once you're right.' Gibb was conscious that it was very cheap. He mustn't lose his temper, mustn't demean himself.

But Menderez paid no attention. 'Well?' he asked again.

'Fifty thousand pounds,' Gibb said.

'Indeed?'

Kenneth Gibb began to rise. He had discharged the bargain; he was safe.

'Sit down,' Menderez said.

'I think I've done all you require of me.'

'Sit down, please.' Menderez drew his hand along his cheek. He was very well shaven, but the gesture suggested that he doubted it. 'How did you find out?'

Kenneth Gibb said stonily: 'I don't think you can ask me that.' He was very stiff indeed.

'Why not? How do I know you're not just guessing?'

'I suppose you don't.'

'But I must. Change the question, then. Who told you?'

'Damn it. ...'

'All right, I concede you that. I respect your nice feeling.' Menderez didn't sound ironic. 'But this you must answer.' He considered for a moment before he asked: 'When did you last see Mason?'

Gibb, very surprised, heard himself say shortly: 'Mind your own business.'

'I'm doing just that. Yesterday you came to see me, but you hadn't what I wanted. That's twenty-four hours ago. It wouldn't be impossible to check Mason's movements for twenty-four hours. Or yours. . . . Whom you had met, and if it was each other.'

'Check them, then. If you must.'

'You can see it would be easy?'

'I dare say it would.'

'And yet you won't answer me?'

'Certainly not.'

Very slowly Menderez's expression began to change. At first it was astonished; then horrified; then utterly disdainful. He began to talk again, but not to Kenneth Gibb. To the ceiling he said slowly: 'I thought I was beyond surprise. But I am not. I thought I was beyond contempt. But I was wrong.' He lowered his head again, staring at Kenneth Gibb; he didn't seem to credit what he saw. Finally he said: 'What a nasty man you are! What a swine! What a *basket*!'

Menderez rose as Gibb left, but he did not go to the door with him. He sat down at his desk again. . . . So it was fifty thousand pounds. It was enough after all.

He had still to get hold of it.

He was considering his problem when the telephone interrupted him. A voice he recognized said: 'Señor Menderez?'

'Speaking.'

'We know each other. I've a message for you. Rather an important one. From rather important people.'

'Yes?'

The voice said in a manner which it hadn't quite mastered: 'Certain negotiations are in train. You will understand me.'

'Not how you know. But I understand you.'

'The money in question is not to reach Candoro. Any part of Candoro or any person there.'

'Why not?'

'That is not for me. Your instructions are to obtain this money and to hand it over to us.'

'Why should I?'

The voice returned to its normal London whine. 'Questions', it said, 'are out. We can give you ten days – till Friday week, in fact.'

Menderez drew a careful breath. 'I'm to get it,' he said, 'and hand it over to you, or . . .'

'Or else,' the young man said.

On the steps of the Candoran Embassy Kenneth Gibb had looked at his watch again. It was later than he had supposed, and reluctantly he took another taxi to the Foreign Office. In his room he told his secretary to telephone to Parker's Hotel and to inquire if Mr Mason were in. 'I don't want to speak to him, you understand, or not just yet. But I probably shall in a quarter of an hour. Just find out if he's in.'

His secretary returned almost at once. 'He's out, I'm afraid.' Gibb wasn't looking at her, and she wasn't troubling to hide her expression. It would have surprised him, for he believed that his manner with subordinates was good. He aimed at a certain detachment, but a correct detachment: he would have been astonished to be told that he achieved a bleak and wounding arrogance.

He waited ten minutes, then switched his telephone directly to the exchange. He asked for Parker's and obtained it. 'Mrs Mason, please. Mr Kenneth Gibb calling.'

'Yes, sir. I'll put you through.'

The line clicked and buzzed, for the house-exchange at Parker's was as ancient as the rest of it. Presently he heard Lavinia's voice.

'Kenneth?'

'Good morning.'

'Is it?' she asked.

'I think so. I've been to Menderez.'

'So I've gathered. Francis has just been called to him.'

'Well, that's all right. We're out of the wood whatever happens.'

'You think so?'

'Dash it. . . .'

'Kenneth,' she said, 'come round at once.'

'I can't, I've work, I . . .'

'I think you'd better come.'

94

'What about Francis?'

'Francis is out – I told you. They'll be an hour at least.'

'Tonight,' he began, 'we could meet . . .'

'Kenneth, we're meeting here. And at once.'

'All right,' he said.

It was a deliberate gesture that he didn't take a taxi, one partly to reassure, partly to reassert himself. Instead he caught a bus to Piccadilly, walking the rest. Lavinia was in the smaller drawing-room. At noon they were quite alone there. He saw at once that it was serious.

'Thank you for coming,' she said. He couldn't be certain of irony.

'Delighted. But is it wise? It's the middle of the morning – a bit thick, really, if Francis should come back.'

'He won't for some time. They'll argue for ages.'

'You think he'll agree?'

'I haven't the least idea. I can't say I care.'

Something in her voice arrested him. This wasn't an angel, it was a very worldly woman; and there was something he couldn't put his finger on. In a moment, incredulous, he had it. She was afraid. He put the thought behind him. It was absurd.

She had been drinking, he saw; was drinking still. But she did not include him. Presently, very quietly, she said: 'Kenneth, I'm going to marry you.'

He decided that she was drunk, assuming the uneasy *bonhomie* which was his defence with drunks. 'Whatever you say.' He was altogether too bland.

. . . Marry her – Christ, no! He had desired her and desired her still. She was a beautiful woman, fashionable, well-to-do. She was a conquest. One needn't be ashamed to have possessed Lavinia Mason. But marry her! He had never considered it; he hadn't had to, and that had been fortunate. Lavinia had everything he wanted, not least a husband. But marry her! He wouldn't marry her for – for fifty thousand pounds.

'I wasn't sure before,' she was saying. 'I wouldn't believe it. Now I must.'

He misunderstood her, seizing what seemed an opening. 'Marriage isn't something to rush into. Attractions can be disastrous. All those years together. . . .'

She stared at him, a mask of Medusa. He found that he had

shivered. Her voice cut icily, sober and inescapable. 'Kenneth,' she said, 'you're going to marry me. And you'd better be quick about it.'

'God,' he said. 'God in heaven.' He was conscious that his jaw had dropped. It was a reflex which in crisis afflicted him. He deplored it.

'You'd better be quick about it. I know too much, you see. You're safe from Menderez now. You can forget about that opening you couldn't pay for. You can keep your career – stay in your precious Service. But I'm going to be a diplomat's wife after all. You understand? God help you if you don't. I know you've been to Menderez, you see, and I know what for.'

Kenneth Gibb went home. He telephoned to his office that he wasn't feeling well – a sudden influenza, perhaps; he'd ring again tomorrow. His slippered charwoman was padding about the flat still, and she saw at once that though something was amiss it wasn't influenza. Gibb knew what she would be thinking and he resented it. She smelt a misfortune: there was nothing like a nice disaster. ... Young Willie Smithers at thirty-nine had broken his leg. That George Eady had been sent to Borstal. Mrs Sanders at forty-four had had a miscarriage. ...

Kenneth Gibb shuddered. That wasn't a solution; it didn't begin to be. Lavinia wouldn't hear of it. Besides, it was much too risky. Archaic laws ... If anything went wrong ...

The charwoman interrupted him. 'You look terribly peaky,' she was saying. 'Should I make you something? A nice cup of tea?'

'No, thank you.'

She left at last, a little reluctantly, evidently curious, and Gibb made himself the tea he had declined. If Mason were more cynical ... but he wasn't. Talk about marrying Lavinia and he would probably agree, for he wasn't a dog in the manger or malicious: ask him to divorce Lavinia and probably he would. With yourself as co-respondent. But ask him to collude, play the conventional gentleman, and he would look at you. Kenneth Gibb could see him. He wouldn't be sarcastic, for he would not need to be; he would simply refuse. And for Kenneth Gibb the other was impossible. ... The wife of a friend, hospitality received *en poste*, an official relationship later ...

He wouldn't last a week.

96

Kenneth Gibb's expression was one which his mother would have recognized, for it was that of a child whose favourite toy had broken inexplicably – unjustly. But the child had a fastidious mind, and the phrase which occurred to it distressed him. It was out of the frying-pan into the fire. Gibb frowned irritably. It was a cliché, but unhappily it was all too apposite. Menderez had had him, rolling in the mud; but he had escaped from it. .... For oh, how little time! An hour, or perhaps a little more – an hour and a half at most. Then down it had come again, the deadly dream, nagging, never leaving him. Now it was Lavinia.

He was without illusions about Lavinia Mason. Menderez had spoken of revenge, denying that he had motive for it. Lavinia Mason had. If she fell she would take him with her. She had said so and he didn't doubt her. For once he didn't even try to deceive himself. He knew Lavinia Mason. Lavinia in trouble would pull the pillars down. She wouldn't show hesitation since she would see no cause for it. She'd take him with her.

Of course, if Francis Mason weren't there ...

He began to consider it, deliberately impersonal. *One* could do this, *one* could do that. *One* might dispose of Francis Mason.

He had seen a man die by poison, and in Candoro. It had been at the Masons', at Seven. They had been called in the night by Miguel, old Granclegg's servant. A peon had been dying in his quarters, and Miguel, who wasn't a man afraid of simple words, had said he had been poisoned. They had all gone down there – Clegg Mason in an overcoat thrown on his pyjamas, Francis, and Kenneth himself. Only Lavinia had stayed behind. Even then, Gibb remembered, she had had a separate bedroom. They hadn't woken her.

The scene had been one which had lived with him – the tiny room, crowded and shockingly hot, the kerosene lamps, flame-steady in the windless night, the peon on a sagging string cot. He had been more than half-Indian, and his women had stood round him in a silence more moving than tears.

Clegg Mason had looked at him once, asking a question or two. Then he had shrugged.

Presently the priest arrived: it had been much too late for doctors. Granclegg had held the man, speaking softly in dialect. With an utter dignity the peon had taken his hand and kissed it. The priest had done his business.

97

When the man died they left.

Clegg Mason strode back to the ranchhouse. They had almost reached it before he said: 'Poison, I think – no, I know. A killing, anyway.'

'I'm afraid so,' Francis said.

'A killing. And that means another. Not immediately – not in this generation maybe, but in the next. They never forget. So not in my time . . . but in yours.'

Francis did not answer.

'There'll be an autopsy, of course – the police will open him. I know what they'll find. I've seen it before. Twice.'

'Twice too often.'

'Not that they'll pin a thing on anybody, and not that it will matter. Most of them know, but no one will speak. Instead they'll wait. . . . Had he brothers?'

'Two. And a son. He's fifteen now.'

'So they'll give him two years. Two years till manhood.'

'Three, perhaps.'

'Three at most.' Clegg Mason strode on, silent and withdrawn. On the veranda steps he said unexpectedly: 'I like them. I respect them.' His smile was grim. 'At bottom there's nothing between us. Injure a Mason and sooner or later . . .'

He had stalked to his room again.

Kenneth Gibb rose from his chair, pacing his little sitting-room. This was England, not Candoro. Killing a man. . . .

Or having Lavinia break you. Not Menderez now – Menderez was discharged. Lavinia . . .

There was a party at the Candoran Embassy on Saturday. He had accepted a week ago, and had thought of excusing himself, since he did not wish to meet Menderez again. But now he was glad he had not. Francis Mason was certain to have been asked.

CHAPTER TEN

FRANCIS MASON had taken Clare Kendrick to dinner, and not to Bloch's. Instead they had gone to a Spanish restaurant not tiresomely meticulous about apparent cleanliness. But the food was excellent: he could give her the *paella* which he knew she loved, and now she was eating it with relish. Neither was talking a great deal, partly because neither, happy in each other's company, had need to; and partly because both thought it wise to skirt the subject which in both minds was uppermost.

So that she surprised him when without warning she broke the ice. Her face was impassive as she asked him suddenly: 'What will you do about Seven?'

'How much do you know?'

'Nothing, really. I know what's happening, but not how far it's gone. I can guess Menderez gave you a price ... and that you didn't agree to it.'

'Not quite. I gave him one, but he didn't accept it. It's deadlock.'

She dropped her eyes, attacking the *paella* again. 'You could have Six.' She spoke not looking at him, hurriedly, her mouth still full of rice and chicken.

'I don't know what you mean.'

She raised her eyes, swallowing like a child caught in ill manners. '*Sua casa*,' she said.

He was astonished and very moved. *Sua casa* – it was a conventional politeness, but with Clare it wasn't. Six would be hers and she was offering it him. And she meant it. People, he thought sardonically, seemed always to be offering to stake him, people whose stakes he wouldn't take or couldn't. Lavinia, for instance: she had offered to set him up in England. He'd see her to the devil before he were beholden to her. . . . And now it was Clare.

Of course it was impossible.

She seemed to read his thoughts. 'I don't think Lavinia will ever go back to Candoro.'

'I know she won't, but ...'

'But what?' She smiled, unembarrassed now, serene. 'I'm not asking you to marry me, you know.'

He found he was blushing.

'Six will be mine in time. Father has a sort of nephew, and I dare say he'll do something for him. But he'll never leave him Six. This nephew's called Guy, and he's a Civil Servant with four children. They live at Woking. He'd never come to Six: father would never leave it him.'

'Maybe. Just the same...'

'Just the same father wants Six to go on. I couldn't do that alone. I'd want a manager.'

'You could marry one,' he said.

She wasn't angered. 'Some nice Candoran? Some well-bred nobody? Somebody who'd marry property? I'm adopted, suspect...'

'Be quiet,' he said 'Be quiet.'

'I won't be quiet – I'm not a child. I'm making you a business offer.'

'You're shaming me.'

'I didn't intend to.' She sighed unhappily. 'Men ...'

He called the waiter and settled the bill. 'Come on,' he said. She went with him unprotesting. They found a taxi and Francis directed it. 'Come on,' he said again. 'Let's dance.'

He had ideas about dancing and defined ones, for it was something he loved. But the band was important. He disliked the uneasy compromises of the ordinary commercial dance-band, and for intellectualized jazz he had a brisk contempt. . ... Some socially connected trumpeter blowing intensely and with a lip not quite firm. Some smoky, ill-lit cellar, arty and artificial. Beards, dirty jeans, stale hair, gulpings, and moans in the dark, the sort of stuff which, when it was recorded, earned bouncy little articles in one of the Sunday newspapers.

He hated it.

He knew what he wanted, and he wanted two things: he wanted to dance and he wanted to listen. For the former he knew a band, quite a small one, quiet and properly pulsive. In New York they were common as sparrows but in London a rarity. He had never decided why. And to listen to he asked the best. He knew a dance-hall, quite a modest one, where the band was good for dancing, and, by great good fortune, they had as guests ... Well, he would show Clare what they had as guests.

He directed the taxi to the Lydda. The driver looked mildly

surprised, for he was thinking that neither of his fares had quite the air of regular patrons of the Lydda. He was a fatherly man, anxious to be helpful. 'Strangers to London?' he inquired.

'More or less.'

'The Lydda, eh? If you don't mind my saying so, it isn't quite your cup.'

'We'll risk it,' Francis said.

In the taxi Clare was evidently excited. 'I've never been there but I've always wanted to.'

'It isn't what you read about in newspapers. No fights, no tights. It isn't exactly a Palais, but it's just as well-conducted. And very much better bands.'

'Room to dance?'

'You have to get on quick. When there's a crowd they close the floor.'

'Sensible Lydda.'

Francis paid the taxi at the door. Clare noticed that he seemed to know his way. So this was how he spent his evenings. She had often wondered. His evenings without Lavinia.

They walked into the Lydda's pleasant asepsis. It was bright but not garish, warm but not oppressively. There were tables four or five deep round a floor not too enormous and not too small. At either end were bandstands, one of them empty. Francis found a table, ordering lager beer. The English band was playing, and the lighting went cosily pink.

They went on to the dance-floor. Francis danced beautifully. Like many men who spent long hours on horseback he was light on his feet; he had a natural rhythm. Clare wasn't in his class, but she was competent. The essential she had, for she loved the act of dancing. He held her a little tighter, feeling her against him, firm and quick-footed. He was thinking it was a pity Lavinia had never danced properly. She could have, he decided, but the inhibitions had been too complicated. In Lavinia's world dancing – proper dancing – was suspect. There were contemptuous little gags about the palais style. It simply wasn't done to dance too well: one might be mistaken for a professional. Move more than a foot at a time and you were risking a show-off; dance unaffectedly, showing you enjoyed it. . . .

Obviously you were an ill-bred person. The night-club shuffle was *de rigueur*.

Presently they sat down, drinking their beer. The houselights went out suddenly, and a single spot ravished the empty stage. Eight Negroes drifted on to it, sucking at cigarettes, cigar stubs. They sat down quietly in the merciless light, fondling their instruments – trumpet, clarinet, two trombones, guitar, double bass, a man at the piano and another at the battery. All would have died before appearing with a saxophone. They stared into the dark hall with a soft arrogance, for they were famous men. They ground their smokes out under large expensive shoes. The pianist threw a run or two, the brass blew a meditative toot. And suddenly, without visible signal, they were away. Nothing of lead-in. One moment they were silent, eight Negroes in a very bright light, the next they had a wild divinity. They had a technical perfection which would have earned them places in any Philharmonic, and something else which would not. The glorious scarlet row strode out from the stage. It was Beethoven's Equali in a delicious high fever, it was catharsis, total release, it was . . .

Francis Mason had shut his eyes. Clare, smiling, watched him.

Later, in the taxi back to Clare's flat, Francis felt for a cigarette with his free arm. He pulled from his pocket not his case but an unopened letter. It fell on the taxi's floor. 'Good heavens,' he said.

'What's the matter?' Clare was half-asleep again.

'It's a letter from Granclegg. The porter passed it out as I was leaving the hotel. I'd forgotten all about it.'

Clare Kendrick hid a smile. She was a woman and she was flattered. 'You'd better read it.'

Francis picked the unopened letter from the taxi's dirty floor and Clare found a torch in her handbag. He slit the envelope, reading his grandfather's beautiful clear script. He handed her the letter. 'Read it.'

'If you wish,' she said politely.

'I do wish.'

Clare read the letter, leaning against him; she shook her head. 'I suppose it wouldn't do.'

'It wouldn't do at all,' Francis was definite.

'Has he spoken of it before?'

'Yes, in a way. Not seriously, though. He'd never stand the journey.'

'He might. He's very tough.'

'It'd be a disaster if he suddenly arrived. It's a delicate matter and ...'

'And Granclegg isn't a delicate man.'

He laughed a little shortly.

'You think he's serious?' she asked.

'More serious than before.'

'What are you going to tell him?'

'I'll have to stall, but I've stalled before. I'm always stalling.'

'Yes,' she said. 'Yes. ...' She didn't sound wholly convinced.

Francis caught the overtone of doubt. 'You'd let him come?' he asked. He didn't believe it.

'No, not yet. I'd think about it, though. Until next week – wait till next week.'

'But Clare, it's absurd. Granclegg doesn't go round things; he charges them.'

'Which sometimes works,' she said.

He took her hand but he did not answer. It was out of the question. Granclegg would go baldheaded at it; Granclegg would kill any tiny chance which still survived. Granclegg ... *las boleadores!* Granclegg would make a *boleadores* of it. Or the other, the shorter word which, partly for euphony and partly otherwise, they never used.

Kenneth Gibb had been taking a day away from the Office. He had telephoned again after his breakfast, explaining that he was still a little rocky. .... Yes, he supposed it had been influenza. Today was Friday, and a long week-end would put him right. It hardly seemed worth coming in, but of course he'd be there on Monday. His secretary had made sympathetic noises, though she wasn't particularly fond of her master. The rest, she had said, would do him good.

Kenneth Gibb had agreed, though he intended to spend his day in anything but resting. He was in fact very busy indeed, watching his own activity with a detachment which he found convenient. It was convenient to be standing outside all this, this buying of drugs and a few simple tools. Once he had been a chemist, a technician, and it was this chemist, not the diplomat, who now walked London, buying here and buying there, always where he wasn't known. What he was buying wasn't a poison, but he did not wish a counterhand to remember a purchase unusually big. He could do the concentration himself – he still had the skill for that, and in any case it wouldn't be complicated. A simple retort, a tube or two, a solvent, a bunsen burner . . .

He bought them carefully at different shops.

For this other Kenneth Gibb, this chemist, had considered it very carefully. It was a break that Lavinia Mason was an addict of Tom Ormonde's little tubes. Francis, one must assume, was not, but that in a sense was an advantage too. He would have easy quite unsuspicious access, and it was notoriously easy to take an overdose of an unaccustomed drug – unaccustomed and, by definition, resorted to only in stress. There had been hundreds of such cases. Coroners made little speeches about them. The public must really read the label carefully lest an overdose . . .

Francis Mason was going to get an overdose.

Kenneth Gibb, counsellor of embassy, watched this other Kenneth Gibb approvingly. He seemed to think lucidly. He had rejected anything fanciful – public analysts were much too clever, autopsy an art much too advanced to take a risk with. There was supposed to be a South American poison which . . . The chemist Kenneth Gibb smiled tolerantly. Mysterious South American poisons he deprecated. There were poisons in South America, no doubt – native and typical poisons. Native and typical, and by that the more easily identified. And there was a group which, administered with wine, left little but a stomach full of vinegar. Little but, to the properly skilled, that fatal something. Or there was that book – what was it called? – Glaister's *Medical Jurisprudence and Toxicology*. A small knowledge of it had hanged more men and women than the public hangman. No, it was stupid to poison and hope to conceal it – stupid and dangerous and crude. Instead you took an authorized drug, a fancy barbiturate as it happened, and you concentrated it. Then you slipped it in Francis Mason's drink. It wouldn't taste or smell, or not very much. Not after a drink or two, and not after you'd finished with it. It was certain to be champagne or champagne cocktails at the Candoran embassy. Champagne had a pretty strong flavour, and in any case Mason smoked like a chimney. He couldn't smell a manure heap.

And afterwards? With any luck there wouldn't be an afterwards. There would be another little speech by yet another little coroner, and a funeral which Kenneth Gibb, the Counsellor Kenneth Gibb, would attend. With any luck there wouldn't be an afterwards, and if by some chance there were, some discovery of motive, some suspicion . . .

Then the essential was not to behave suspiciously, not to be too clever. No dropping your burner into a lake, no hiding your glass in some suburban wood. Smash the lot; chuck it boldly in the dustbin. In forty-eight hours it would be God knew where, the burner, in pieces, deep in some nameless dump, the broken glass, dust probably by now, beyond even the detective of fiction. The Borough Council was very efficient with refuse.

Kenneth Gibb finished his shopping and went home. In the familiar flat the familiar Kenneth Gibb came for a moment uppermost. He made himself a cup of tea. He wasn't excited – in a sense he wasn't even interested, for he wasn't concerned. But he was thinking that this other Kenneth Gibb, the chemist one, was really quite efficient.

With only ordinary luck he was going to pull it off. Tomorrow night.

Sir Godfrey Henn wouldn't openly have admitted that he thought of a minister of state as 'just a politician'; he and his senior colleagues had subtler resources to point a superiority which they were too honest not to recognize, too well-disciplined to define. They spoke of 'our masters' and they did it beautifully, their tone neither contemptuous nor ironic. But the educated ear caught its nuance precisely. Men like Sir Godfrey Henn were public servants: ministers – the Foreign Office had three by now – ministers were government and came and went with governments. Sir Godfrey Henn sat on, experienced, wise, continuity personified. Ministers did the talking and the Sir Godfreys the solid work.

This evening, as he walked into the courtyard, he heard himself hailed. It was the second minister of state, and Gog knew him only slightly since he worked to another. He walked across to the official car.

'Can I give you a lift? Can I drop you?'

'It's very kind of you.' Gog told him where he lived.

'That isn't out of my way. Jump in.'

Gog climbed into the car, relaxing but warily. Mr Tester was a new appointment, and his reputation was – well, Sir Godfrey would have called it insecure. He made up his mind very quickly

but his average of mistakes was high. Now he said irritably:
'What a day.'

'It wasn't worse than usual on my side,' Gog was smiling.

'You don't take Candoro, do you?'

'Not directly. I see the dispatches, of course.'

'And they didn't scare you?'

'If I scared,' Gog said, 'I'd be dead by now.'

'I wish I'd your phlegm.'

'Candoro's been touch and go for at least a year. Lucky it's in
South America, not Europe.'

'Yes. I agree it's not our worry, or not in the first place. Nevertheless we don't want to see it go red.'

Gog said reflectively: 'It's impossible not to admire them – the
sheer political competence. Beside them the Americans are children. And we . . .'

'Yes?' Mr Tester asked. He spoke a little sharply.

'We used to send a cruiser. Nowadays that isn't conspicuously
successful.'

The Minister frowned. He had been concerned in a recent dé-
bâcle and had barely survived it; he returned the conversation to
Candoro. 'It's obviously serious.' he said. 'Only a question of
time. It isn't as though there were an effective alternative. . . . How
long would you give it?'

Sir Godfrey Henn shrugged. 'Perhaps a fortnight,' he said.

CHAPTER ELEVEN

At the Candoran Embassy it was a party again. The lights were brighter than the guests, but the guests weren't dim: champagne had dissolved the more distressing of their inhibitions. On the walls the minor Spanish masters stared in astonishment. The saints smiled insensate smiles of bliss, the martyrs, almost smugly, paraded appalling wounds. The guests went on drinking, and His Excellency had already been removed.

Francis Mason was chatting to Clare Kendrick when he noticed Captain Jay. Jeremy Jay was hovering, and in the matter of Jeremy Jay Francis's conscience wasn't as clear as it might have been. On an earlier occasion he had shamelessly cut him out, and he wasn't ungenerous. He murmured something to Clare, starting to drift away.

Clare too had seen Jay and she wasn't in the mood for him. He bored her severely. She had had two drinks already, and two was her normal ration. But with Jeremy in the offing ... She picked up the drink which Francis had left. It was a fresh, full glass, and she drank perhaps half of it. Then she stopped suddenly; she glanced about the room – Jeremy Jay had been intercepted. Very carefully she smelt her drink, sniffing it, a wary animal. She was conscious that she was very white. She looked about the room again: nobody seemed to be noticing her. She backed against the wall, dropping her glass in a potted palm. In the party's din the noise as it broke was nothing. Then she walked quietly to the door.

She was terrified – terrified and fighting a mounting panic. She hadn't much time and she knew it. At the embassy's door there was trouble about a taxi, and she held herself grimly. Finally she walked for one, sighing as she found it. She directed it to her flat.

She hadn't a doubt what had happened. Like Kenneth Gibb she had seen a man die of poison, but not in the dignity, almost the peace of the peon on Seven. This had been on Six, and the poison had been corrosive. It had been noisy, unrelievedly horrible. Clare shouldn't have been there – wouldn't have been except for accident. The memory had never left her.

In her taxi she shuddered. ... It probably wasn't that. Her mouth wasn't burnt and she wasn't in pain. Then it was the other sort, the sort where you slept and never woke. Unconsciously she straightened her back. Then she tapped on the taxi's partition.

'Yes, Miss?'

'Be quick. Please be quick.'

'I'm doing the best I can.' The driver was offended.

... A doctor – who wanted doctors? They only asked questions, they only wasted time. You had nothing to tell them, nothing of what they would expect. They might think you hysterical. They'd send you to hospital – for observation. *They* would observe and *you* – you would sleep. You'd sleep and sleep, and next day ...

At her flat Clare paid the taxi, not waiting for her change. She found her key, frightened that her hand was trembling. For she had work to do.

She set about it, cool still, but only just. She found wine and salt and warm water from a kettle, mixing them and drinking. It was the emetic of her race. Whilst she waited she made strong black coffee. That too she would need, and time might be against her. At any moment the thing might bite, and when it did ...

She caught her breath sharply, holding herself again, reining imagination.

In the little bathroom, delighted, she was violently sick. But she wasn't satisfied. She drank more wine and water and shudderingly retched again. Then she went to her bedroom. She opened the window, for warmth she feared. And comfort too. She fetched a straight-backed chair and put it by the open window. The coffee, in a thermos, went on a table beside her. For a moment she collected her thoughts. ... No, she had done what was possible. There was nothing more. She was alone now, like sick animals she had often seen, desiring only solitude.

She almost smiled. She wasn't an animal, there *was* something else. Clare said a prayer and crossed herself.

She settled to fight for her life.

It was thus that Menderez found her. He had seen her leave the party and he hadn't been worried: indeed he had hidden a smile. He approved. An evening with Francis Mason was better than any diplomatic cocktail party.

Later he had noticed that Francis Mason hadn't left. Well, a little competition wasn't a bad thing.

Later still he had remembered her face as she left the room. She hadn't looked like a woman keeping an agreeable engagement.

When he returned to his flat he telephoned to Clare's. He didn't receive an answer. Very well, he decided, she was out still. She was very attractive and there were a million young men in London. He went to bed but woke in the small hours, surprised to discover that he was worrying. He telephoned again: again no answer. Deliberately he began to dress. After all, he was responsible for her; he was her official superior and something else, something important. She didn't know it and he hoped she never would. She was Clare Kendrick now.

He found her upright in her chair still, the coffee gone, half-conscious but fighting still. She smiled at him but did not speak.

Menderez flamed into action. He went to the telephone first, ringing a doctor, a personal friend; he spoke with a precise urgency which the doctor, a good one, recognized. Then he carried Clare to her bed. He felt her hands and her pulse; he looked at her eyes and suppressed a whistle.

'I ought to make you sick.'

She managed speech. 'I've *been* sick.'

'Thank God for that.'

The doctor did much as had Menderez but more professionally. A Scot, he wasted few words. To Menderez he said: 'A barbiturate, I think'; to Clare, very quietly: 'Do you take sleeping pills?'

She was speaking more easily now. 'Never.'

'Odd – very odd.' The doctor turned to Menderez. 'You say she's been sick?'

'So she tells me.'

'It's a very strange language, English. . . . "Been sick" – now what would you think that meant?'

'What are you asking me?'

'The mood of the verb.'

Menderez was silent, and the doctor looked at the coffee pot.

'That at least is transitive,' he said. 'It didn't make itself.' He reflected a moment, seeming to come to a decision. 'Not that it's any of my business professionally. She'll live, and I know you're diplomats. She'll live. Putting it undiplomatically, she's saved herself. But I can help a little.' He took a hypodermic from his bag, charging it carefully; he gave Clare the injection, watching her.

109

Satisfied, he turned again to Menderez. 'She'll be all right. Better stay with her, though. Good morning.'

'Thank you,' Menderez said. 'Thank you doubly.'

'I'm a physician. I try to *save* life. Good morning again.'

Menderez heard the noise of his car diminishing down the street.

He took Clare's hand, watching her revive, watching the dawn creep up the wall. It was Clare who spoke first. 'Somebody tried to poison me.'

'Don't talk, he said. 'Just rest.'

'I'm all right now. But worried. . . . Who would want to poison me?'

'Perhaps they didn't.'

'You don't think I tried . . .?'

'No I do not.' He hesitated, inspecting her. 'Are you really fit to talk?'

'I *want* to talk.'

'Then tell me what happened – whatever you can remember.'

She told her story simply, not taking her eyes from his impassive face.

'You were with Francis when this happened?'

'Yes.'

'You're sure it was his drink?'

'I saw him put it down.'

'He hadn't touched it?'

'No. It was full.'

'Did you see where he got it from?'

'No.'

'You wouldn't,' Menderez said. 'You wouldn't be meant to.'

'Menderez, what are you telling me?'

'The obvious. Francis Mason had a poisoned drink. You drank it, or some of it. Lucky you don't smoke. Lucky you've a dog's sense of smell.'

'Lucky you came here. . . . Why did you come?'

He didn't answer directly. 'I don't think it made that difference. You'd have lived, I think: the doctor made it easier. You'd saved yourself, you know.' He rubbed his unshaven chin. 'Clare, you're a very brave woman.'

'But why did you come?'

'I was worried.'

110

'But why?'

He considered carefully before he said: 'We're all very fond of you.' He was thinking that that was true: they were all very fond of Clare Kendrick. And Menderez especially, for he had reason to be. He took her hand and kissed it, not as a lover, nor formally. The gesture was fraternal.'... Old families could be very stupid and very cruel. Their father had been a decent man, but he had been a prisoner of his name and environment. Under the pressure, the final pressure of his clan he had collapsed. A widower of a loveless marriage, he hadn't dared marry Clare's mother. She had been a splendid woman too, handsome and bold and free. Her race had been as old as Menderez's, but not the same.

Menderez hid a smile, a grim one. Clare Kendrick was half his sister. Also she was a love child. She had the advantage of him.

But she was speaking again. 'What will you do now?'

'Look after you.' He smiled again. 'Especially at parties.'

'But you said it wasn't me they meant to kill.'

'Accidents will happen,' he said vaguely.

'Menderez ...'

'Rest,' he said. 'Just rest.' He looked at her again and, satisfied, rose. In the tiny kitchen he brewed more coffee and brought it into the bedroom.

'Though you can sleep now,' he told her. 'You've earned it. I'll come back at lunchtime and cook you something.' He grinned. 'I'm a terrible cook. Have you any rice?'

'A little.'

'Proper rice – not English grocer's?'

'Of course not.'

'I can manage that. I'll start it now. It's Sunday and the shops will be shut, but I can bring a chicken. Cold, I'm afraid. A bottle of Rioja, fruit ...'

'It's a feast.'

'Now sleep,' he said. He took her hand and kissed it again.

Menderez walked back to his flat through the increasing dawn. He bathed and shaved, listening to his housekeeper busy in the kitchen. The bacon, as always, smelt delicious. Bacon and eggs was one of the nicest things in England, one of the Anglo-Saxon's contributions to the good life. It was Menderez's opinion that they hadn't been many.

He ate his breakfast with relish. .... An extraordinary people. This Gibb, for instance – who would have guessed he was a killer?

Menderez finished his breakfast and lit a cheroot. Then he crossed to his desk, taking paper and a pen. He was smiling, for he was amused at himself. He wasn't a fanatical admirer of his British colleagues, and it tickled him that he should so easily have caught a habit of theirs. They grossly overdid it, but in its way it wasn't a bad one: Get It On Paper.

He began to write quickly:

A. The drink was meant for Mason: that is reasonably established.
B. It had been poisoned with what must have been an overdose of some sleeping drug. That's what the doctor was suggesting. I wouldn't think that could have been done simply by putting sufficient tablets into a glass of wine and hoping they would dissolve, and tastelessly.
C. So that some technical knowledge would be necessary.
D. Which Kenneth Gibb has, or at least had once.
E. As Gibb has also motive for killing Francis Mason.

Menderez read this through, laughing aloud. It wasn't a bad Minute; all the facts were there and lucidly; it could perfectly go forward to the next man up the ladder. Where there would be nods of approval for a job well done. It wouldn't be counted against it that it advanced the matter nothing – not a step. It was in perfect form but perfectly ineffective. That wouldn't matter.

Take A, B, C, and D – they were simply the facts. E alone was important, and E was precisely what Menderez mistrusted. He read it again:

E. As Gibb has also motive for killing Francis Mason.

But had he? Lavinia Mason was his mistress, but Gibb wasn't the man to marry a mistress. The Kenneth Gibbs didn't marry mistresses. And if that was a generalization, a guess impossible to be sure about, there was something more concrete – Menderez's own instinct. He was prepared to trust it. The Kenneth Gibbs of the world might or might not marry mistresses, but Kenneth Gibb – not an abstraction, this, but a man he knew – Kenneth Gibb wouldn't kill.

Or not without motive much more immediate. Menderez could

imagine only one; he thought ill of himself even to have considered it.

He discovered a mounting anger: Kenneth Gibb had nearly killed his sister. That this had been an accident merely made him angrier: the affair had been an affront to family. And it had been Francis Mason whom Gibb had intended to kill, and that was an aspect also personal. A dead Francis Mason was useless to Menderez and Gibb must know it. To kill him or to try to was a double-cross, personal, and calculated. Menderez smiled savagely, remembering that once he had warned Kenneth Gibb against the double-cross; Gibb couldn't complain if now ...

Menderez would have to keep an eye on Kenneth Gibb.

Indeed he would. There was a convention that poisoners became too confident; that poisoners poisoned again. Menderez didn't credit it, but here it was irrelevant. For Kenneth Gibb wouldn't be poisoning again: Saturday's attempt would be simply a false start. He must be happy at his good fortune. After all, nobody had died – not Mason, but equally not some other guest, not some servant swigging left-overs. Clare had destroyed her drink and in doing so opened the race again. Menderez chuckled grimly. He must have a word with Clare this afternoon. She wasn't a talker, her mother's people had too much respected truth to dribble it away in chatter, but he would speak to her – make certain of silence. That doctor wasn't talking either – he had been clear about that ... Keep quiet yourself. Keep your eyes open. Wait developments.

Menderez didn't doubt they would occur, nor that he could use them. They were in fact his only chance of fifty thousand pounds from Francis Mason. His lean face set in a quick disgust, for the weapon offended him. ... Warn a man – save his life; tell him you'd saved it; then ask him for money again. ...

It was wholly degrading – only the end excused it. Candoro ...

He spent the afternoon with Clare, dozing in a chair as she slept after lunch again. He left her at six o'clock, comfortable now, and walked to his own flat. A hundred yards from it a man slipped quietly from the mist and joined him. Menderez acknowledged him. 'Good evening.'

'Good evening,' the young man said.

'You must find your job a cold one.'

'I'm what they call an outside man. I work outside.'

'Come in for a change.'

'No thank you. I haven't much to say. .... We gave you till Friday, you know.'

'What of it?'

'Nothing,' the young man said. 'Nothing very much. Only that it's Sunday. That's five days left to get it.'

He smiled and the fog swallowed him.

CHAPTER TWELVE

CLARE KENDRICK woke on Monday perfectly restored, but she did not go to the Candoran Embassy. Menderez had told her not to, and she was grateful for a day away from work. For, like Menderez himself, she had thinking to do. She didn't tackle it with Menderez's lucidity, far less on paper, but her decision was as clear. She didn't consider herself a clever woman and she was therefore free to use her advantages – a perceptive instinct and the wisdom to trust it. To Clare Kendrick the situation was obscure but the action required of her self-evident: Francis Mason was in trouble and she must help him.

To begin with, Menderez was inexplicable. He was after the Mason money – he had admitted it – but he had rather more than hinted an unwillingness to see it in Romero's hands; he had dropped an innuendo, talking obliquely, as men would; then, when she had given him opportunity to explain, he had slid away from her. Clare smiled – tolerant, a woman. Menderez was playing at something. He wouldn't or couldn't tell her, but he hadn't been able to resist a hint of its existence.

And that wasn't the end of it. Menderez was playing at something which, disguise it as he might, meant bleeding Francis Mason. But somebody was playing at something else: not to blink it, they were trying to kill him. Clare hadn't even considered that this somebody could be Menderez himself. Menderez might kill – she could imagine it – but never that he would kill by poison. It was inconceivable, not Menderez at all. But somebody had attempted it, and Menderez had told her that the somebody could try again. He had sworn her to silence and she hadn't demurred, for she could see that there was nothing concrete to go on, nothing for the incomprehensible British police. Nevertheless there was more than enough for Clare Kendrick. Francis Mason was in trouble – yes, and danger – and she must help him. She didn't know how to, and in those circumstances there was an admirable rule: you told your elders, those you respected. They might not be able to help you but they were entitled to the chance to try.

Clare Kendrick put on a hat. From a mirror a determined little

face stared back at her. She walked to a Post Office and wrote a
cable to Charles Kendrick. She didn't try to condense it.

SOMETHING HAS HAPPENED HERE BUT I DO NOT KNOW WHAT
STOP NO PROGRESS SEEMS TO HAVE BEEN MADE IN A MATTER
CLEGG MASON WILL KNOW ABOUT STOP I AM NOT HAPPY ABOUT
FRANCIS BUT LEAVE YOU TO DECIDE WHETHER TO SPEAK TO
CLEGG STOP LOVE STOP CLARE

Clare read this through. She expected that it would be intercepted but she was reasonably confident that it wouldn't be
suppressed. Romero's censorship would read it and perhaps
delay it for instructions. But she had drafted carefully: to the
Romeros, she had decided, the message might even seem helpful.

It had also occured to her that it might easily lose her her job.
She hadn't weighed that for a moment.

At priority rates the cable cost a good deal of money. The clerk
was dourly conscientious, asking if the I's were really necessary,
and the STOPS. Clare Kendrick said they were. ... Then the
wording could be cut down. Clare didn't wish it cut down. The
clerk shrugged irritably. His private politics were covetous Left,
and he was thinking that these upper-class foreigners had much
too much money still. For an Englishwoman, happily, this sort of
wickedness was almost impossible.

Clare paid for her cable and walked home. By Candoran time
it would arrive very early in the morning: she could expect an
answer by the evening. She cooked a late breakfast and composed
herself to wait.

She would have admitted it wasn't easy.

Francis Mason had been to a theatre with Lavinia. It had been
a theatre in south-west London, one which he hadn't visited before and both of them, though for different reasons, had had mis-
givings: Lavinia hadn't been quite certain that this theatre was a
place to be seen at, though a first night was always a first night;
Francis had simply feared boredom. He was fond of the theatre,
but aware that there were people who would consider his tastes
old-fashioned, even barbarous. He liked a play to have a beginning and a middle and an end; he liked to spot the crises, to recognize a craftsman at his business of constructing craftily; he liked

a firm ending, to leave the theatre with that tiny scar on consciousness which meant he had been moved. He knew that there were people who talked crossly about commercial theatre and the well-made play; he knew their opinions but he did not care for them.

So that he had been mildly apprehensive of the Moberley, and in the event correctly. The play had been something to do with a Negro slum in Johannesburg. Most of the cast had been black, a garrulous exception a white South African who had fallen in love with a Negro. There had been ravings about apartheid, rantings about the colour-bar elsewhere. Francis Mason liked neither, and he would have agreed that a man who knew his business could possibly have made a play of them. But not this unhappy woman whose naked propaganda bored him. She had made a speech when the curtain fell, and Francis had squirmed for her in a sweating embarrassment.

Now he was in the taxi back to Parker's, sitting beside Lavinia. He had noticed that she had been quieter lately – quieter but not less tense. . . . An unhappy woman – he couldn't hate her. Waste, he thought surprisingly, waste and frustration. Her child had died. . . . She had a man's appetite for life, a man's gusto to seize it. But none of a man's training. That foolish, wicked mother! They should have put her to work, made her stick to it, given her some skill: nursing, commercial art but not the other sort, teaching – it wouldn't much have mattered. Instead they had sent her to a fashionable secretarial college: she had a diploma to say she was a secretary. Why, she couldn't even type decently. She had drifted from job to job, an amateur, a changeling, resigning at the first reproof. Then home again to much too easy commiseration. All that vitality – wasted, cramped by the pettiest sort of snobbery. Unconsciously he shook his head.

'What's the matter?'

He thought quickly, lying for once almost smoothly. 'I was thinking about the play.'

'You didn't enjoy it?'

'Frankly, not much.'

'Nor did I. I suppose it was significant, whatever that means, but nothing seemed to happen.'

'It didn't.'

She laughed, for a moment at ease, 'I liked the audience, though.'

'Yes?' He was surprised.

'Yes, indeed. You should have watched them in the intervals. About a third was enthusiastic or pretending to be; another third was bored; and the rest watched the others to see what they should do.'

'You're pretty observant.'

'Perhaps. When I want to be.'

In the taxi there was a moment's silence, almost the silence of friends. She broke it, saying quietly: 'Francis . . .?'

'Yes?'

'I thought you might be asleep. Francis . . . You know we talked about Seven.'

'I remember you said you wouldn't go back there.'

'No. . . . You were good about that. I think perhaps you understood.'

'I understood,' he said.

'Then I made a suggestion and you turned it down.'

'You offered to set me up here.'

'And you declined. Then I was pretty bloody.'

He didn't contradict her.

'I'm sorry about that,' she said simply.

'You must realize that Seven . . .'

She laughed unexpectedly. 'But I do. I realize it better than you. While Granclegg lives Seven is Francis Mason. I can see that; I sympathize. But when he's dead . . .'

In the taxi's near-darkness Francis could see her white shoulders. They went up once and down again. He asked her quietly: 'What are you getting at?'

'If Granclegg were dead, how would you feel about Seven?'

'It's my living,' he said. The words astonished him.

He heard her laugh again. 'When we first came over, a fortnight ago – would you have said your living?'

'I honestly don't know. You're talking – doing something. . . .'

'Something important.'

'To you,' he said resentfully.

'No, to you. I'm making you think – think of Seven. Do you want it? Can you see it – here in London? Really *see* it?'

He was silent.

'There's money here, you know.'

'Not that again,' he said.

118

'You misunderstand me – I didn't mean mine. There's fifty thousand pounds, and if Granclegg were dead ...'

'He isn't.'

'But if he were?'

'You're a witch,' he said. 'You see too much.' But he spoke without anger.

'I'm your wife. I've been a very bad one, but tonight I'm helping you.' He saw her shrug again. 'Tomorrow I'll be the same old bitch.'

'Go on.'

'You give yourself away, you know. We talked of this before and you spoke of an obligation – an obligation to Granclegg. To Granclegg, you said – never to Seven. And we talk about Seven tonight again, and the word you use is a living.'

'Hell,' he said unhappily. 'Damnation.'

'You want to be sure. You *must* be sure.'

He did not speak again till the taxi was almost at Parker's. Then he said slowly: 'Suppose we had the fifty thousand – fifty thousand free of Seven. Suppose we stayed here ...'

'We?'

'I'm your husband.'

He heard her laugh once more and on a note he didn't recognize. For a second, moth-light, her hand brushed his own. 'There are some things', she said, 'I wouldn't do to you.' Her voice changed to normal again. 'Now pay the taxi, please.'

The young man was reporting to Peter Amadeus. Amadeus was saying smoothly: 'You'd better tell me what happened. All of it.'

'It went comfortably enough – no blood, no violence even. Lucca and Brutus didn't have a chance to do anything silly. The man collapsed at once.'

'He was frightened?'

'He was frightened all right. He told us the whole story.'

'You think he was telling the truth?'

'I'm sure of it.'

'How?'

'When they're frightened enough,' the young man said, 'they usually tell the truth.'

'Hm. ... That's a generalization, you know: it isn't true of

119

Orientals. An Indian, for instance, will always give the answer he thinks will please you.'

'This animal isn't an Indian.'

Amadeus stroked his considerable jowl. 'You were there?' he inquired. 'Yourself? All the time?'

The young man nodded.

'Then I'm inclined to accept that you're right. From Lucca or Levy, no. They have their modest uses but they're hardly sensitives: I wouldn't back their estimate of what was truth.' Amadeus smiled amiably. 'But yourself now . . .'

'I thank you.'

'Not at all. Now tell me what he said.'

'He broke down at once. He babbled. Lucca and Brutus Levy don't look very nice perhaps – hardly gentlemen.' The young man paused before he added: 'Menderez has been in with those others all along.'

'He has, has he?'

'Yes. This refugee man was high in the comic opposition before Romero caught him. He was lucky to escape. As he stands – in London and penniless – he amounts to precisely nothing, but he's still a contact. That's what he was doing with Menderez – contacting him, passing him a message.'

'From what you've just called the comic opposition?'

'Exactly.'

'Why was he doing that?'

'I told you. Because Menderez himself is deep in it.'

'I see. . . . Which hardly fits with working for ourselves.'

'You do the thinking,' the young man said.

'But I do not need to. Menderez was suspect, so we arranged to test him. Now he isn't suspect any longer – he's against us. What that man said . . .'

'It's evidence,' the young man said cautiously.

'In our profession it's proof.' Amadeus rose, pouring drinks at the sideboard. Returning to his chair he said: 'Menderez has been working for those ineffectives all the time. Menderez has been *taking* us. Menderez is walking about still, knowing too much. Menderez is intolerable.'

'We needn't tolerate him.'

'No.' Amadeus's mouth was suddenly a slit again. 'No,' he repeated, 'we needn't.' His face relaxed slowly. 'But we must give him till Friday. I promised him a week.' He began to laugh quietly. 'And afterwards, after Friday ...'

The young man looked thoughtful. 'Lucca and Levy?' he suggested.

'No. Somebody more polished. Antonio ...'

'Antonio's a Castilian.'

'I know.'

'That means he's a knife man.'

'I know.'

'Rather messy, don't you think?'

'Tell him not to make a mess.'

The young man considered again. At length he said: 'It'll take a day or two to arrange. ... Not before Friday in any case – Friday evening.'

'I'm quite agreeable.' Peter Amadeus reflected. 'After all, I gave him till Friday evening, and I'm a man of honour.'

The young man stared at him. Amadeus seemed perfectly serious.

It had been half past four when the telephone rang in Clare's flat. She didn't run to it but very nearly. She drew a deliberate breath, steadying herself, making sure there was a pencil and a scribbling block beside the telephone. Then she took the receiver, writing the words carefully.

No reason alarm Masons but Clegg no condition face journey England. However am seeing him afternoon and cabling again. Could come myself if your reply more definite. Father.

Clare read this twice, then made herself very strong tea. She was trying not to cry. She respected her father and loved him. But she was a realist. Charles Kendrick couldn't help; Charles Kendrick was shrewd and a very nice man. A very nice man was useless: it was far beyond that, and six Charles Kendricks wouldn't add up to Granclegg.

It was eight hours later when Francis Mason paid off his taxi. He walked with Lavinia into Parker's and, as they passed the desk, the night porter held out an envelope. 'In a moment,' Francis told him.

He saw his wife to her room and went downstairs again.

121

In the almost deserted sitting-room an ancient waiter brought him beer and sandwiches. He opened the envelope.

ARRIVING LONDON AIRPORT FRIDAY MORNING 0200 FLIGHT 167 STOP MEET STOP BOOK ACCOMMODATION ONE NIGHT PARKER'S BUT LEASE HOUSE AT BLENDON IF POSSIBLE STOP CLEGG

... So he'd lost patience at last. It wasn't his sort of affair and he would realize it – after all he had first sent Francis. But if matters were getting nowhere, clearly drifting, then Clegg Mason wasn't the man to drift with them indefinitely. Francis smiled, for he knew his grandfather. ... Diplomacy – bah! There were other and older weapons and Clegg Mason would try them. Francis was conscious that he held one at least: counter-blackmail. Menderez and Clare Kendrick – Granclegg knew about that. Put him in a corner and he wouldn't hesitate to use it.

Francis folded the cable deliberately, putting it in his pocket. His emotions were surprising him. There was relief that he was no longer responsible: Seven was still Granclegg's and he was coming to fight for it; but there was something else which astonished him. Lavinia, he thought wryly – she was very observant and, in her queer way, wise. Lavinia would have the word for this other emotion; Lavinia didn't pull punches.

Francis Mason sighed. Lavinia, he decided, would have called it indifference.

Of course that was absurd. Seven was home, Seven. ...

Seven seemed a long way away.

Francis looked at his watch. It was half an hour after midnight, but he walked to the telephone. Menderez had given him his private number and now he dialled it. There was a moment's delay before the answer.

'Hullo.'

'Francis Mason here.'

'Delighted.'

'I hope I didn't wake you.'

'No. ... What can I do for you?'

'We were talking, you remember – business. I can't go on with it. My grandfather arrives by air. On Friday.'

There was a silence before Menderez said quietly: 'I see.'

'I'm out of it now. Seven is his.'

122

'Yes. . . . Nevertheless I'd like to meet him if I may. Not at the embassy. I'll come to him.'

'That's kind of you. He's pretty old.'

Francis heard Menderez chuckle. 'But still Clegg Mason.'

'I very much hope so. . . . Come here, then – to Parker's.'

'Whenever you say.'

'Could you have lunch on Friday?'

'I should be honoured,' Menderez said. It was evident that he meant it.

CHAPTER THIRTEEN

FRANCIS MASON met the aircraft in the small hours of a bitter February morning. He had arrived at Heath Row an hour before the plane's estimated time of arrival, and it was as well that he did so, since almost at once his name came over the public address system. In the almost empty hall it echoed portentously. 'Mr Mason, Mr Francis Mason. Will Mr Francis Mason please go to the room by Channel Fifteen. The small room beside Channel Fifteen. Mr Francis Mason. . . .'

Francis discovered something between a consulting-room and a miniature hospital. There was a worried airline official, a doctor, and a sleepy nurse.

'Mr Mason?'

Francis nodded.

'I think your grandfather is on 167. I'm afraid I've bad news for you.' The official handed Francis a pencilled message and Francis read it.

'I see.'

'I can't be sure,' the doctor said, 'but it sounds like a heart attack.'

'I wouldn't be surprised.'

'He had something wrong with his heart?'

'He had angina.'

The doctor frowned. 'Why on earth they let him on board. . . .'

'You haven't met my grandfather.'

'No. But we've done what we can this end. The aircraft will come right up, and we've fixed it with Customs and Immigration. There'll be an ambulance. We'll get him away at once.'

'Is he conscious?'

'Oh yes.'

'Thank you,' Francis said. He had private doubts about the ambulance.

At half past two they walked to the freezing tarmac. Officials stood aside sympathetically. A gangway, manned, was ready and, as the plane cut its engines, its crew ran it quickly alongside. For a moment of drama nothing happened; then the door opened.

Clegg Mason stood blinking in the flaring arcs. Miguel held

him on one side, a steward on the other. The gangway would take only two abreast, and it was on Miguel's arm that he began it. Very slowly, one hand on the banister, Miguel holding him, he fought his way down. His face was a livid grey, his breath came with a pain which the knot of men below the gangway shared instinctively. The descent took a very long time. At the bottom two orderlies waited with a stretcher. The ambulance backed up, its doors already open.

Clegg Mason's feet were at last on England.

He managed a smile for Francis, moving his eyes at the stretcher. 'What's that?'

Trying to be matter-of-fact, Francis said quietly: 'That's for the ambulance.'

Clegg Mason fought for a shallow breath. 'Damn the ambulance.'

'But Granclegg. ....'

'Do you think I'll die in some hospital? Haven't you a car?'

Francis caught the doctor's eye. His shrug was almost invisible.

They carried him very carefully to Francis's hired limousine. Francis sat beside him, Miguel and the doctor on the folding seats. On the journey to London he spoke only once: 'Where's Lavinia?'

'I didn't know you would be ill. I didn't wake her.'

Clegg Mason did not answer.

In bed at Parker's he rallied a little. To the doctor he said politely: 'I shan't be detaining you long'; to Miguel, in Spanish: 'Sit me up decently. I won't die lying.'

Miguel, gentle as a woman, bent his broad back. Clegg Mason was a big man, but Miguel moved him like a baby. He set him upright, propping him with pillows. Then he stepped back to the bottom of the bed: that was his place until called again. He began to weep silently, his rosary clicking through strong peasant fingers.

Clegg Mason said to Francis: 'I'm afraid this isn't helping.'

'Don't think about that.'

'But I must. .... You know where it is?'

'The bonds?'

'What else.'

'I know where they are.'

'Then don't pay any duty on them, or not on more than half. I put it in both our names.'

'All right.'

'You've got a key?'

'You gave me one.'

Clegg Mason shut his eyes and the doctor began to move to him. He stopped as he opened them again. For a moment Clegg Mason's voice was normal, deep, and strong. 'No mourning,' he said. 'Promise me no mourning. I should hate that. I haven't lived badly. ... No need to annoy people.'

'I promise.'

'Bury me decent but bury me quick. No stone.' Clegg Mason looked squarely at Miguel. 'Miguel,' he said, 'servant, old friend, *amigo* ...'

Miguel broke down. Through his tears he said: 'Master, a priest ...'

Clegg Mason said something about priests, something final. He shut his eyes again, and the doctor watched him. When he opened them his voice was weaker. 'Give me a cigar.'

'Granclegg ...'

'Give me a cigar.'

Miguel produced one, cutting it with a formidable knife. He wiped his lips carefully and lit it; he put it between Clegg Mason's, but the old man's hand went up to it. 'Damn it, I can smoke still.' He pulled once or twice and then began to cough. His face twisted hideously, but he held the cigar still. At last he had his breath again or what was left of it. Now his voice was very small.

'Give me a drink.'

'Granclegg. ...'

'Give me a drink. Brandy.'

Miguel found a flask as he spoke. He poured brandy into a tooth glass, holding it up, showing it, waiting.

'That's not a proper drink.'

Miguel doubled it. He gave the tumbler to Clegg Mason, stepping back again. Clegg Mason raised it. 'Seven,' he said, 'Seven. ...'

He drained the glass and for an instant sat smiling.

The tumbler fell shatteringly on the floor, the cigar on the counterpane. Almost at once it began to burn it. The doctor picked it up. Clegg Mason was dead.

At ten o'clock, four hours after Clegg Mason's death, Francis telephoned to the Candoran embassy. He was connected with Menderez, then said briefly: 'I'm afraid I must put you off for luncheon. My grandfather died this morning.'

It was a moment before Menderez answered. 'I'm truly sorry.' He sounded truly sorry. 'Now I shall never meet him and I'd always wanted to. A splendid man. A splendid life.'

'I'm glad you feel that.'

'And now – now that you own Seven?'

'It's difficult,' Francis began. He had been surprised, the last few hours, just how difficult it was. Seven without Granclegg ... It was his living, but politically it was at risk. He could settle with Romero, but that wasn't buying much. Ten thousand, he had thought – fifteen at most. And after Romero?

After Romero the deluge. Plus fifteen thousand down the drain.

But Menderez was speaking again. 'But Seven's still there, you know. And so's Romero.'

'And after him?'

'Gaze in your crystal ball.'

Francis said reflectively: 'Once I mentioned sequestration. It could happen; it's a factor.'

'It could happen – in the future. No man knows that. But a great many things could happen at Seven, and now. Tomorrow if Romero lost his temper.'

'I wouldn't deny it.'

'It's a sort of equation,' Menderez said. 'Money by time by guess at the political future. There's one unknown at least. I realize that.'

'The sort of equation where there's more than one answer?'

'Oh, certainly. ... But we might agree on one.'

'I'd like to see you,' Francis said. 'Tonight if you can manage it.' He was thinking that he would get it over and be glad to. One way or the other.

Menderez seemed to hesitate. 'But your grandfather ...'

'Granclegg swore us to no mourning. He always loathed it.'

'I'd like to come to the funeral, though. Officially and, if you'll let me, privately as well. There weren't many like him.'

'You're very kind. It'll be some time tomorrow. I could let you know tonight.'

'Come about six, then – here, to the embassy. Most of them will have gone, and we can talk quietly. I've a bottle.'

'About six if I can, but we're pretty busy. You'll understand if I'm a little late.'

'I'll wait for you. Don't worry.'

Menderez too put down his telephone, resuming the conversation which Francis had interrupted. It was with Luis. Menderez had sent for him to ask for help. He was conscious that he needed it; he had assumed a responsibility and he was very far from sure that he could carry it alone. Kenneth Gibb was a killer – so far an unsuccessful one, but he could try again. Menderez thought he would. He had sworn Clare Kendrick to silence, which did not trouble him since to have gone to the police could hardly have protected Francis. There was nothing to convince a policeman – he might easily have laughed at you – and even if he hadn't the police could hardly dog a diplomat from rout to rout. For that was where it would happen – at another party. Gibb wouldn't risk an intimate occasion: elimination, the search for the man with motive would be far too easy. He was free to try again, and by precisely the same means. He wouldn't know that he had almost killed Clare Kendrick: on the contrary he would be congratulating himself that, if Francis hadn't died, nobody else had either. ... Yes, it would again be at a party.

And there was one on Saturday, one at the Anglo-Candoran Institute.

Menderez had sent for Luis. He was friendly with him; once in Candoro he had done him a kindness; Luis was seventy now, and more; but he hadn't always been seventy, and when he wasn't he had known things and done them too. Some very unusual things. He was just the man Menderez needed.

Now he sat in Menderez's armchair, a wizened, oldish man, but growing in stature visibly as the story unfolded. This was his meat and he knew it: authority flowed back to him, outwards again to Menderez. 'I agree,' he was saying crisply. 'Gibb wouldn't ask Mason to lunch *à deux* and poison him at his club. He'll try the same again.'

'I'm relieved you think so too. I don't know what we'd have done if you'd felt he might try anywhere.'

'No, he'll choose the big occasion – plenty of people and so plenty of suspects.' Luis shook his head. 'If there *is* any suspicion,' he added. 'On what you tell me Gibb might get away with it.'

'And there's a party tomorrow, you know.'

Luis looked shocked. 'Tomorrow? But Clegg Mason died this morning. I heard you speaking of it. Francis Mason won't be going to parties tomorrow.'

'He will, though.'

'It's an outrage! His grandfather barely cold. . . .'

'You didn't hear all of it. Clegg Mason hated mourning – men of that sort often do. He made them promise not to observe it.'

'I'd have promised too,' Luis said. 'Anything to a dying man.'

'And broken your word?'

'In the circumstances – unhesitatingly.'

'Well, Francis Mason won't.'

Luis shrugged. 'Protestants', he said sadly, 'are capable of anything. Any indecency, any scandal.'

'I don't say I don't agree, but there it is. Francis Mason will be there and so will Gibb.'

'And so', Luis said, 'shall I.'

Francis Mason had been delayed by the arrangements for his grandfather's funeral, and it was nearly eight before he reached the Candoran embassy. He had said that he might be late, but this was very late, and he was anxious lest Menderez should have abandoned hope of him. But Menderez was there still. He received him smiling, waving apologies aside. 'But it *is* a bit late,' he said. 'Should we go to my flat?'

'With pleasure.'

They walked into the faded splendours of Wilton Crescent, across Knightsbridge and into the park by Albert Gate. The night had turned surprisingly warm, and the sudden warmth had had what in February was the inevitable result: it was decidedly foggy and getting foggier. Francis said conversationally: 'The park will be pretty thick.'

'Don't worry, I've a torch. Not that we shall need it, though. I walk this every night; I could do it blindfold.'

Francis was silent, for he had his doubts, and, passing the Dell, Menderez turned the torch on. 'It's worse than I allowed,' he said. But he was confident still, crossing the Serpentine Road. Six paths fanned out before them, and Menderez took the left-most.

Straight through to Victoria Gate,' he said. 'Nothing to it.' In the gathering murk the preposterous gas-lamps were visible but no more. Francis stopped for a moment, slipping off his overcoat, hanging it on an arm. 'Too heavy to walk in,' he explained. 'I made a mistake – I should have brought a raincoat.'

In the gloom Menderez nodded. Somewhere to the left, vaguely below them, the Serpentine stank sourly. They were entirely alone.

They began to climb the rise, Menderez switching the torch, his iron-shod heels clicking on the tarmac path. Presently, near the top, he said: 'Tea-house over there.' He flicked his torch to the right, but its beam vanished in ten feet. Francis could feel that they were going down again – feel but not see. On his left a lamp glowed bluely. 'Police station,' Menderez said. 'Filthy night to be a policeman.' There were lights again, right-handed now, and Menderez explained them. 'Ranger's Lodge,' he said. 'Watch it for a bit. It's steeper than you think.'

They had walked eighty yards when it happened. Menderez didn't follow it, or not at first. He saw that a man had stepped from behind what he knew was an ancient pump; he saw an arm come up and, as it crossed the torch's beam, the sudden glint of steel. Then he fell in an untidy heap – Francis had pushed him. He fell on a single hand. He wasn't thinking but by instinct he still held the torch. He heard Francis Mason's voice say urgently: 'Keep that torch on him.'

Menderez, rising, did so. He whistled softly, for what he saw surprised him. A man stood uncertainly, holding a knife; he was staring at Francis Mason and he didn't know what to do.

For an instant Menderez moved the torch to Francis. He began to laugh quietly, for he could understand the other's uncertainty. . . . You hid with a knife in the fog and you struck at an unarmed man. You struck at an unarmed man, and instead . . .

Instead Francis Mason was standing quite still, his weight on the balls of his feet. In his hand was the *facón*, the *gaucho* knife, all fourteen inches of it. Menderez couldn't think where he'd been keeping it. His left arm was bent, held rather low, the overcoat wound round it once, the bottom trailing. 'Keep that torch on him,' he said again.

The two men stared at each other silently. They were eighty yards from a major police station. In the fog they might have been on Mars.

Menderez said softly: 'What shall I do?'

'Nothing. Stand still. Keep the torch on him.'

Menderez chuckled. He had never been any good with a knife, but he could recognize the expert. As boys they had fought every Sunday – his brothers and the senior peons' children. The knives had been wooden, their points carefully padded. It had been sport but a serious sport. ... The long Spanish shawl wound on the bent left arm, its loose end trailing, blinding the stroke, tripping, like Francis's overcoat; the circle of interested elders, encouraging but solemn as churchgoers; the modest bets, the knowledgeable praise and blame. He hadn't been any good at it but ...

But clearly Francis had.

The two men stood quite still, the stranger puzzled, trying to decide. Presently he began to move. Menderez said quickly: 'He's coming in again.'

'Keep quiet.'

There was a blur of explosive action. An arm came up again but not from Francis. Instead he seemed to drop his left, raising it again in a sudden jerk. The other staggered, not quite falling. For a second he was quite defenceless. Francis's right hand started to move.

Menderez saw that he had checked it. His cool voice said level-ly: 'He isn't first class.'

Menderez began to laugh again. He wasn't any good with a knife but he knew about knife-fighting. It wasn't unlike that English game, squash rackets. Menderez had played it, and he knew that if you were just that little better you could concede the earth – bisques, six points, owe what you like. And still you won. He said to Francis Mason: 'Will you kill him?' He spoke un-emotionally; he didn't feel concerned, but he was curious.

'What do you think?'

'Well ... England, you know. The body – they're bound to find it. Footprints – all that. They might trace us.'

'It's up to you, of course. I don't think he was after me.'

'You'll kill him if I say so?'

'Naturally. He tried to murder you.' Francis sounded surprised.

Menderez had an instant to decide that he had been right about Francis Mason. Francis Mason was amiable and fair-minded: it was Menderez's opinion that in his private life he was a trifle too tolerant. But now he was none of these. He was holding a frightful knife and he had the advantage of at least one class on an assailant. He could kill him quite easily and, if Menderez asked him to, he would. Heredity, Menderez thought – this was Clegg Mason's seed. The king is dead: long live the king.

He said solemnly, for he was trying not to laugh again: 'Perhaps it would be wise to leave him.'

'Just as you say.' Francis was evidently considering. He was watching the stranger still, his eyes not moving from him. He spoke to him softly in Spanish: 'Next time I won't be fooling.'

He began, very slowly, to move forwards.

For a second the other hesitated, then started to back away. Francis did not follow him. In half a dozen paces he was lost in the fog.

Francis said to Menderez: 'What now?' He was speaking Spanish still, and Menderez wondered if he realized it.

'Four hundred yards to the Bayswater Road.'

'What's between it?'

'A sort of wood on the left. Bird Sanctuary. The path just skirts it.'

'We'll keep away from it. What's on the right?'

'A tree or two. Then open ground to Victoria Gate.'

'I see.' Francis had made up his mind. 'We'll keep to the right. You go first. Keep switching that torch. Shout at once if you see anything.'

'What about you? Behind me, no torch . . .'

'Don't worry about me.'

'But . . .'

'Let's move,' Francis said.

Menderez began to move. From time to time Francis touched his shoulder. Menderez could feel it was a left hand touching him. He grinned. Francis Mason was right-handed.

At Victoria Gate cars were feeling their way out from the Ring Road, their headlamps barely visible. Francis stopped, slipping back into his overcoat. The knife had disappeared. 'We were going to your flat,' he said.

'Thanks to you we're still going.'

In Menderez's flat he mixed large drinks. Over his own, bowing, he said formally: 'I owe you my life.'

'It was nothing.'

132

'It was something – something you don't know.'

'What's that?'

'It's altered everything.' Menderez rose from his chair, pacing the room, speaking very quickly. He told his story simply, as he saw it but without apology. 'So,' he concluded, 'so you see I was cheating you. Naturally I can't go on with it.'

'I'm not sure I follow. You say our money wouldn't have reached Romero?'

'Never through me. Never.'

'Instead you'd have taken it? And given it to your friends?'

'So I intended.'

'And these people, these people you've been fooling: you haven't been wholly successful. They're suspicious of you; they demanded the money themselves; they gave you till tonight, and when you didn't produce it...'

'They were quick enough,' Menderez said.

'They were that.' Francis Mason sipped his enormous whisky and Menderez watched him. Presently Francis said reflectively: 'This party you've been trying to fool – what are its chances in Candoro?'

'Uncomfortably good.'

'And your own friends'?'

'Speaking as now I must – they're bad.'

'But,' Francis said, 'they'd be the only chance, the only hope for Seven. I've some money, as you know. Now that I know the truth I've half a mind ...' He smiled disarmingly. 'To lend you some,' he said.

'That's impossible.'

'Why?'

'I'd have fleeced you for Candoro – stolen from you. Now that you've saved my life I can't *accept* from you.'

Francis said something in Spanish and Menderez smiled. 'No,' he said, 'you're not wholly Candoran. Not like me.'

'Then suppose I still want Seven?'

'The outside chance to save it? After what I've told you? I wish I could believe you but I can't. You're not a fool. Keep your money – use it to start again. You can do that and I cannot. I won't drag you with me.'

'You're dragging nobody.'

'I won't let you take the risk. I cannot, now.'

Francis Mason finished his whisky. 'You're very proud,' he said. 'I like it. Watch out for yourself. Good night.'

'Wait . . .'

'What for?'

Menderez hesitated; he himself was wondering what for. Francis Mason had told him to watch out, and he should be telling Francis the same. Kenneth Gibb was trying to kill him, and the simplest warning . . .

He couldn't give it. Mention that Gibb was trying to kill him and Francis Mason might guess why. Also he would guess that you knew why, and that would cut deep in Mason pride. He had just saved your life, turning your shameless plans against you. That wasn't without irony. But you were under an obligation: this of all moments wasn't one to wound. Menderez sighed. 'Nothing,' he said. 'Good night and thank you again.'

'Good night.'

Menderez sat down. He knew this couldn't go on: sooner or later he must warn Francis Mason. But not tonight. He was in debt and for his life. Tomorrow he might repay it – tomorrow at the Anglo-Candoran Institute. Afterwards they could meet as equals.

Tomorrow evening . . .

Peter Amadeus had been dining at his favourite restaurant. It was late when he left it, but the doorkeeper found him a taxi. As it began to move the door on the street-side opened quickly and another man slipped in. Amadeus recognized him. He shut the glass partition between cab and driver, and the newcomer began to speak. But not in English. Shaking his head he said: 'That wasn't very clever.'

'What wasn't very clever?' In the hierarchy of Amadeus's employers the man in his taxi wasn't very high. Amadeus wasn't afraid of him.

'Trying to kill a man and failing. I'm not to be misunderstood, though. We will assume that this Menderez had crossed you; we will assume you thought it necessary to eliminate him. We don't quarrel with that – you are permitted to maintain your disciplines. But you are not allowed to fail.'

'How did you hear of this?' Amadeus, now, was less assured.

'A man called Antonio came to us.' In the taxi's dim interior

the other smiled. 'Antonio is scared of you – I do not wonder. But he is much more scared of us. And, if I may say so,
rightly.'

'Where is he?'

'We have him,' the newcomer said coolly. 'We'll keep him for
a bit.'

'Is that wise?'

'That is for us.'

Amadeus reflected before he asked: 'Then what are your instructions?'

'But surely they are obvious. You tried to kill Menderez –
that's your own business and we do not inquire of it. But you
tried to kill Menderez and failed. That *is* our business; that is very
dangerous indeed. To all of us.'

'I quite see that.'

'Then act accordingly. Finish the job.'

'I'll do my best.'

'I advise it,' the other said. 'I advise it most strongly.' He rapped
on the driver's partition and the cab slowed down. As he got out
he said: 'We pay for the best and we expect it. We don't care for
blunders.'

It was midnight before Menderez contacted Luis, but he came
to the flat at once. He listened with an increasing tension, his
grey face hardening. When Menderez had finished he said simply: 'You were lucky.'

'I know it. . . . What now?'

'It's difficult. I know about them, naturally. They're very well
organized – very formidable indeed.'

'I can't stay mewed in this flat for the rest of my life.'

'It may not be long if you don't. Keep away from the park,
though – that's obvious. And don't take taxis – they've a thing
with taxis. And don't go out at night.'

'I must.'

'Why? When?'

'Tomorrow night. We're going to the Institute, remember.'

'*I'm* going,' Luis said.

'I must go too.'

Luis sat still for some time. 'In a matter of conscience,' he
began.

'In a matter of conscience.'

Luis shrugged. 'Very well. I'll call for you in a taxi.' He smiled a little grimly. 'In a taxi which I will select myself.'

CHAPTER FOURTEEN

KENNETH GIBB had spent his Saturday morning in south-east London. It was an area quite strange to him: that was the reason for his choice – he would be an alien there, he wouldn't be recognized. It would have been dangerous to make again just the same purchases at just the same shops. Instead he took a bus to the Elephant, walking along the Walworth Road, turning down side-streets, collecting what he wanted piece by piece. It went into a briefcase very easily. He knew just what he wanted; he had, he reflected, experience to guide him.

He finished his shopping, looking around him curiously ... So this was south-east London. It wasn't likely he would visit it again.

In that he was mistaken.

The Anglo-Candoran Institute was a very odd body indeed. It dealt in Fellowship and Culture, the capitals almost audible. It had brought a Candoran pianist to England and had arranged a concert for him. He had been unbelievably bad. It had organized an exhibition of contemporary Candoran painters. Nobody had gone to it. The Institute hadn't been deterred, for it was comfortably subsidized. Wealthy Candorans, though reluctantly, felt it wiser to disgorge; an English organization even queerer than itself made it an annual grant. This the taxpayer footed since he hadn't in practice the option. So that the Institute didn't lack money – only horse-sense. It was extravagant pointlessly but it watered its gin. Its parties were a byword.

Tonight's was no exception. They had hired a hotel in what was w 1 but only just, and, since the occasion was a big one, the Institute was running to champagne. It had bought it cheap. There had been a fire in Dockland, and somewhere in the salvage a dozen cases of a champagne which had been indifferent before the fire. Parboiled it was indescribable. But the Committee hadn't hesitated. After all, this wasn't some vulgar beano. It was the spirit which counted – international cooperation, the common heritage of the arts ... I'm so glad you agree, dear. Materialists who noticed what they were drinking ...

137

They could quietly go to hell.

Menderez and Luis arrived early. Menderez was impressed that in an almost empty room Luis was at once inconspicuous. A waiter offered him champagne and Luis took a glass. He sipped it; looked puzzled; put it down again. In an instant he had vanished again against the background of the quickly filling room.

It was half an hour before he saw what he expected. The Institute had been mean about waiters, and in the press they were overwhelmed. People were helping themselves, carrying drinks to friends. Kenneth Gibb had a tray of them and he was walking towards Francis Mason.

In six quick strides Luis was beside him. 'I'll take the tray.'

'No, thank you.'

Luis did not answer. He had put on his spectacles and was inspecting the drinks. There were just four glasses. On the outer corner of the tray, the corner Gibb would offer, one drink was a little different. A tiny sliver of lemon peel floated on its surface. It was almost invisible. They weren't champagne cocktails.

Luis took two glasses from the tray, one of them with lemon peel. For an instant he turned his back, then faced again to Gibb. He was holding two glasses of champagne, and neither had peel. He held them before Kenneth Gibb. 'Have a drink,' he said pleasantly.

Gibb was very white. 'No, thank you,' he said again.

'It might be the easiest way. I know what's in one of these glasses and what isn't in the other. I shall take them both away, and there are clever men ...'

Gibb began a movement at the glasses, but Luis was too quick. 'No,' he said, 'not so easily.' He stood very still, watching the sweat break dully on Gibb's forehead.

Lavinia Mason was suddenly upon them. 'Kenneth,' she began; but she stopped at once, staring at him. 'Why, what's the matter? You look like a ghost.'

'I ...'

'You need a drink and so do I. Your very kind friend has two.' Smiling, very quickly, she took a glass from Luis, draining it, handing the empty back to him. 'Thank you,' she said. 'I needed that. You've saved my life.'

Luis stood like a statue. He didn't know what to do. . . . Warn her? She wouldn't believe him. Insist? There would be instant uproar, an unseemly scene, a scandal. Gibb wouldn't help him – he wouldn't dare. Luis couldn't tell the truth except to Menderez, and Menderez . . . ?

Luis looked about the roaring room. Menderez was talking to Francis Mason.

He'd be a drunken old man, disgracing himself. They would hustle him away, lock him up for the night, and next day . . .

He gave Lavinia a stiff little bow. Then, holding the other glass, he walked away. He went to the lavatory and locked the door. The smell of a recent faeces fought with some disinfectant. Luis didn't notice it.

He was a very old man. He fell on his knees, to pray, but the movement continued. He hadn't meant it to, but suddenly he was beyond intention. Later one or two people tried the door: one even banged on it, waiting a little.

Soon he too went away.

CHAPTER FIFTEEN

A FRIGHTENED chambermaid woke Francis Mason on Sunday morning, and he went at once to Lavinia's room. He had seen death often enough to have an instinct for its presence. He waited for the doctor. The doctor made his examination, then turned to Francis. 'I'm afraid there's no hope,' he said.

It was his formula.

'I didn't think so.'

The doctor began to pack his bag. Not looking at Francis he asked: 'Tell me, did she take sleeping drugs?'

'She did.'

'Habitually?'

'Yes.'

The doctor said quietly: 'I'm afraid she took too many.' He shut his bag and turned again to Francis. 'There'll have to be an inquest.'

'I suppose so.'

'Not that there'll be unpleasantness. A child could see she was an addict and I'm not a child. I see a lot of this, you know – I wish I didn't.'

'Thank you,' Francis said.

He walked dumbly downstairs to a breakfast he didn't want, and in the lobby he was hailed by Menderez. Menderez was very gay, a flower in his lapel. He had made his decision and the aura of a huge relief shone from him happily. He hadn't seen Luis since the party, but Francis Mason was all right – he had checked that by telephone earlier – and if Francis Mason was all right then Menderez could talk. He *ought* to talk. There would be difficulties in telling Fráncis that Kenneth Gibb was trying to kill him, delicacies when it came to the question of motive. Menderez had decided that he must ride them: what he could ride no longer was the possibility that Gibb might succeed. If Gibb succeeded, Menderez withholding warning . . .

In effect he'd be a murderer himself.

Francis said dully: 'What can I do for you?'

Normally Menderez was sensitive, but this morning the release of his decision blunted him; he waved a hand airily. 'I just came to see you were alive,' he said. He had considered the remark, and it hadn't seemed a bad lead-in.

But he saw at once that he had said something. Francis's face set like a stone. 'Come with me,' he said shortly. 'You owe me an explanation.' He turned on his heel and Menderez followed him.

They went to Francis's bedroom. Francis pointed at the chair, sitting himself on the unmade bed. 'Now,' he said icily.

Menderez was at a loss. He could see that something was wrong, something much more serious than what perhaps had been too frivolous an introduction, but he hadn't an idea as to its nature. He looked at Francis Mason, but he hadn't relaxed. Menderez at last said quietly: 'I do owe you an explanation. That's what I came about.'

'Well?'

'Kenneth Gibb has been trying to kill you. He's still trying.'

Francis Mason's expression did not change. 'But that explains nothing.'

'May I start at the beginning?'

'If it helps,' Francis said.

Menderez glanced at him. Francis sat in a cold, a frightening calm. It was Menderez's impression that for sixpence he would have screamed. He was reining himself, somehow holding on . . .

Menderez began to rush his fences. 'Gibb has been trying to poison you. He made an attempt about ten days ago – at my embassy, as it happens. He failed. Clare Kendrick took your drink, but we got to her in time. That's how I found out. And last night he could have tried again. Perhaps he did, but we were watching him . . .'

Francis said softly: 'You were watching him, were you?'

'Yes, and you're still alive.'

The judge remote on his bench, the judge who had once been a pleasant man called Francis Mason, said in his impersonal judicial voice: 'You congratulate yourself on that?'

'Well . . .'

'May I ask you a question?'

The polite voice hadn't changed.

'Of course. By all means. I – '

'You were talking about Gibb poisoning. What poison was he using?'

'Some sleeping drug – concentrated.'

Francis Mason sat unmoving. Menderez couldn't read his thoughts, but his face appalled him. At last Francis said: 'My wife died last night. Of an overdose of some sleeping drug.'

It was a moment before Menderez understood. He dropped his head in his hands, rocking in his chair. 'Mother of God,' he said. 'Mother of God.'

Francis did not answer him; he was thinking intently. They sat for perhaps five minutes before he spoke again. 'I would like to be sure of this. ... Gibb tried to poison me and nearly poisoned Clare?'

Menderez nodded silently.

'And last night he was after me again?'

'We thought so.'

'And instead of myself ...?'

'Pity,' Menderez said. 'Pity me.'

But the remorseless lawyer's voice went on. 'But you guessed he was going to try?'

Menderez said brokenly: 'Forgive me.'

Francis Mason rose, walking to the window.

God, Menderez prayed, spare me that I need humiliate him too. Let him not mention motive.

But he didn't. Out of the window, his back to Menderez, the hanging judge was talking to himself. 'Lavinia Smart,' he was saying. 'I suppose I never much liked her. But I married her. Lavinia Mason ...'

He returned to Menderez, sitting on the bed again. 'There are questions I could ask,' he said. 'A lot of them. But I don't think they'd help us. Perhaps I could guess the answers.' He sat in a long silence, considering again, and when he spoke he had changed the subject. Menderez heard himself sigh.

'This Amadeus you were talking about on Friday.'

'After you'd saved me,' Menderez said miserably.

'Never mind about that. Tell me about Amadeus.'

Menderez began to talk quickly. 'He's a remarkable man. It's common knowledge who he works for, but he's too well protected to be touched.'

'Protected? In England?'

'Yes. English Protection. It's not like Candoran, you know: you can't bribe a judge, or the police, or not very often; you can't ring up the Public Prosecutor and tell him to drop a case or ...

Not even if you're a minister. It doesn't work like that. It works at discreet little lunches in the better clubs, at golfing week-ends in the country. If you're in any sort of trouble and important enough Amadeus will know of it; he may even have had a hand in putting you there. Then, when anything points to Amadeus, when Security becomes too interested in his affairs, he lets you know. It's all very negative – not the simple corruption of Romero – but it's beautifully sensitive, beautifully effective. And beautifully English. The Establishment – it's an exquisite machine, and by God it hangs together! What the public doesn't know of it!'

'Thank you.' Francis Mason was deep in thought again; at last he said: 'Amadeus told you to get the money and to give it to him. When you didn't he tried to kill you. He must have wanted it damned badly. He must have been desperate for it.'

'It's a possibility,' Menderez said slowly.

For the first time, Francis smiled. 'You know a lot about Amadeus,' he said. 'Do you know his number?'

Menderez gave it to him; he opened his mouth to speak again, but Francis Mason had risen. 'Thank you,' he was saying again. He held out his hand and Menderez took it. He would have liked to ask a question, but he took the hand. Mason had made some decision, something was happening: he, Menderez, wasn't in a position to ask for explanations.

'Good-bye,' Francis said. 'We shan't meet again. Good luck.' He gave to Menderez what was almost a smile. 'From what you've told me you may need it.'

Menderez walked downstairs. He had been mindful of Luis's warning against taxis and had come in an embassy car. He climbed into it thoughtfully, settling on the comfortable upholstery, smiling for the first time in half an hour. He was certain of only one thing: Kenneth Gibb was in trouble. Big trouble. Menderez's smile broadened, for he was remembering a conversation with Kenneth Gibb. Sensible men, he had explained, weren't revengeful, or not without good reason. ... Lavinia Mason, Francis's unfaithful wife. The odds were that he guessed it, but that didn't matter now. For she had been his wife still, a Mason ...

Menderez had seen his face.

He laughed aloud. He detested Kenneth Gibb, he despised him. And he had seen Francis Mason's face.

Peter Amadeus had been astonished when the voice of the man in his taxi spoke to him on the telephone. Cautiously he asked: 'Where are you ringing from?'

'From a telephone box, of course. Yes, I know your line's tapped – you're put on tape, I dare say – and this call could be traced back here. They'd give their pensions to catch me ringing you. We'll have to talk fast. You can guess I wouldn't call you unless it were Emergency.'

'I can. . . . What emergency?'

'You're to see you-know-who at you-know-where.'

'But I was told that never, in no circumstances . . .'

'I said it was Emergency.'

'It must be.'

'And you're to go immediately.'

The telephone clicked once before it went dead in Amadeus's left hand. He observed with interest that its knuckles were bloodless.

He took a taxi along the Bayswater Road, stopping it near Notting Hill, walking left-handed to a very large house. He gave his name and was taken to a waiting-room. A man he had never seen came to him, looking at him carefully, taking him to another waiting-room. He waited again and another man met him, inspecting him even more thoroughly – memorizing him, Amadeus decided. As they went through the door there was the faint click of some electrical apparatus snapping into circuit. Amadeus smiled, for he wasn't armed. He had never carried ironmongery: lesser men did that.

The man who finally received him he knew by reputation but had never met. He sat at a large plain desk, powerful, cropheaded, his squat features more than a hint of Mongol ancestry. He smiled without amusement, indicating a chair, staying seated himself. His English was formally perfect but it wasn't quite English. 'Please sit down,' he said. 'I am pleased to meet you.'

'Delighted.'

'You can guess I wouldn't have sent for you unless it were urgent.'

'I can. I'm pretty sure I was followed here.'

'I haven't a doubt of it.' The man at the desk put his hands on it palm downwards, looking at them briefly. Amadeus could see that he shaved their backs. Presently he said quietly: 'I think this

144

starts when we told you that Romero was blackmailing these Masons and that the Masons had money here. It didn't seem important, but it was in your area, so we informed you.' The powerful face smiled faintly. 'We are always punctilious. We find it pays.'

'I'm grateful.'

'Do you know how much it is?'

'I was never told the sum. Ten thousand, I guessed – fifteen perhaps.'

'I should have thought the same.' There was a pause, nicely calculated. 'We've just heard that it's over fifty.'

'I didn't know that.'

'Well now you do.' The man at the desk reflected. 'There is a connexion between that money and this Señor Menderez,' he said. It was a statement. 'Tell me what it is.'

It didn't occur to Peter Amadeus to lie. 'Menderez has been helping us – you'll know that.'

A nod acknowledged this, and Amadeus went on. 'But recently – quite unconnected with this Mason money – we began to have doubts about Menderez, doubts whether he wasn't really working for the other opposition. So I decided to test him. Any money from the Masons would have passed through his hands in any case, so I told him to get it and give it to me. I gave him ten days, but before they were up, and quite independently again, we discovered that he *was* working for the people we suspected. So ...'

'So you decided to – to discipline him?'

'It seemed essential. He'd been using us; he'd crossed us; and he knew too much for safety.'

'I don't dissent,' the big man said; he stared at Amadeus unwinkingly. 'Now let me tell you something else about Candoro. ... In a fortnight we shall be in.'

Amadeus whistled.

'You see where this is leading us? More precisely, where it is leading *you*?'

'Not fully.'

'I should have thought it obvious.' The man at the desk waited a moment, then said with finality: 'You're to stop that money leaving the country.'

Amadeus said slowly: 'But is that necessary? If we're going to succeed in a fortnight, if that's the timing ...'

The heavy mouth opposite him set grimly. 'I should be reluctant', it said, ''to think you unintelligent. You were about to remind me that if fifty thousand pounds had reached Romero it couldn't have affected our plans. I should have agreed with that. But it's clear, now, that this money isn't going to Romero, and if you were going on to say that even fifty thousand in other hands couldn't do damage . . .' The man at the desk raised an eyebrow. 'Were you?' he asked softly.

'But if we're going to be in within a fortnight . . .'

This was ignored. 'I disagree with you. Fifty thousand is too much. I would concede that it is small arms at most, and in a very few hands at that. Nevertheless it is too much – too much . . . potential. We like to represent these things as perfectly peaceful choices. So you're to stop this money leaving the country.'

'How?' Amadeus asked.

There was a moment of silence before the man at the desk said stonily: 'We never interfere with detail.'

Peter Amadeus had begun to sweat, but he kept his voice steady. 'But you can see that I now have conflicting instructions. The only real hope for this money is that Mason should give it to Menderez still, and Menderez to me. I've nothing on Mason directly. But yesterday you sent Linsky to remind me that Menderez must be made sure of.'

'I did.'

'Then you must see that your orders about Menderez . . .'

'They stand. Get the money from Mason.'

Peter Amadeus heard himself say unevenly: 'I don't think it's possible.'

'I very much hope you're wrong.'

'At such short notice . . . I've no handle against Mason. Safes . . . A total change of plan . . .'

'We make the terms. We give the orders.'

'I'll try,' Amadeus said.

'I wish you success. Sincerely.' The square man's voice was conversational now, saying with a terrifying smoothness: 'Now I have other work . . . By the way, we still hold a friend of yours.'

'Yes?'

'I think he's important, or at least to you. Linsky told you this man was scared of you but much more scared of us. Now I must confirm what Linsky said. Your friend has blundered. So,

146

to speak frankly, have you. But Antonio isn't unconscious of it; he would be glad to retrieve himself. To put it bluntly he would be pleased to oblige us. Professionally. Good day.'

Peter Amadeus returned to his too-carefully furnished flat. He was exhausted and lay down. But he did not sleep; he was much too frightened to sleep.

He knew his masters; he was afraid for his life.

Francis Mason sat down again as Menderez left. He wore a belt below his shirt – money-pouch to the right and, since he was right-handed, sheath to the left. Now he felt for it, drawing the *facón*, balancing it, staring at it reflectively. He shook his head. That would be crude and, as Menderez had once reminded him, this was England: it was certain they would catch you.

He had the outline of a better plan, and now he considered it. He didn't consider his fifty thousand pounds; he was sick at heart of fifty thousand pounds. It might have cost his life – that wasn't quite unimportant – and it had nearly cost Clare Kendrick's. Francis swore savagely. In a sense it had cost Granclegg's, and now, indirectly but inescapably, it had killed Lavinia ... Lavinia Mason. He suspected she was unfaithful and it was certain that she had been a damned bad wife. He couldn't be blamed that he resented it, but he had never learned to hate her. Perhaps he should have, perhaps it would be better if he did. But it didn't matter. She was Lavinia Mason still, his wife, a Mason.

Fifty thousand pounds – this Amadeus must be desperate for it. He'd had some hold on Menderez, demanding the money himself; and when Menderez hadn't broken Amadeus had tried to kill him. Indeed he must be desperate, and clearly he was formidable. He had killers at beck and call and a protection which Menderez had vouched for. Menderez was a diplomat; he understood these things. Mr Peter Amadeus was Somebody in his own world, and Peter Amadeus was in a spot for fifty thousand pounds.

And it was unlucky money: there was blood on it already. Francis Mason didn't consider Seven, for he had forgotten it. There was fifty thousand pounds sitting in London in a safe deposit. In Candoro they would have said that somebody had looked at it, some old woman ...

But it could still be made to work. Granclegg – in heaven one hoped – would approve of that; Granclegg would smile grimly.

This wasn't a pretty thing, but neither was poisoning. This wasn't scrupulous, but neither was Gibb. . . . No, Clegg Mason wouldn't hesitate.

His grandson did, but only for an instant. Francis Mason went to the telephone. The safe deposit company where Clegg Mason had cached his bonds wasn't one of the most well-known, and it was therefore a little less stuffy than its more celebrated competitors. For a special charge it was possible to do business on a Sunday, and Francis looked in his pocket book for a number in the suburbs. A voice, reluctant but unresentful, said finally: 'All right. At three o'clock. Don't forget your own key.'

Francis took a bus to the City. He was aware that he was about to break the law. The bonds weren't his – only a half of them: half was Clegg Mason's estate in England, and Francis hadn't a Grant to it. A bank, if Granclegg hadn't distrusted banks, would probably have refused to hand them over, talking of Death Duty and the Inland Revenue, making a chi-chi, covering itself as banks always did. Francis smiled, for his grandfather's opinion of bankers had been simple: they would always lend you an umbrella when the sun shone. When it went in again they wanted it back, and quickly.

Granclegg hadn't much cared for bankers. He had put his Bearers in a safe deposit, and now Francis and the official used their separate keys. Francis took the single sealed envelope, signing for it. The official counter-locked the empty safe. He made no comment and asked no questions. He was paid to ask no questions.

In the taxi back to Parker's Francis smiled again. He was carrying Bearer Bonds worth fifty thousand pounds and he wasn't an Authorized Depository. He was breaking the law again. . . . Or was he? He wasn't a British citizen or resident in the Sterling Area. He shrugged. None of that mattered.

In his room at Parker's he broke the seal. Granclegg, he saw at once, hadn't done badly. The bonds had been bought in forty-five and forty-six – mostly Shell and de Beers. No British Government stock – Granclegg had been much too shrewd. Francis, consulting Saturday's *Times*, made a rough calculation: at face value there was between ten and fifteen thousands'-worth. But the appreciation had been considerable. Coupons were unencashed and, where they had run out, the talons were in place.

This was good stuff, the best. Francis totted his quick figures, taking the lowest estimate. It couldn't be less than sixty thousand and it might easily be a good deal more.

Peter Amadeus would be interested in sixty thousand pounds. Amadeus would do much for sixty thousand.

Francis made the bonds up again into a curiously shaped parcel. It had to be longer than it was thick or wide, for it must go through a letter box. At the porter's desk he had it carefully sealed. He looked for an address in a telephone directory, then called a taxi.

At Kenneth Gibb's flat he pushed the long parcel through the letter slit.

He returned once more to Parker's, going to the telephone again, dialling Peter Amadeus. To the manservant he said: 'Mr Amadeus doesn't know me, but my name's Francis Mason. If you tell him I'm calling I think he'll speak to me.'

'Very good, sir.'

Amadeus was on the line almost at once. 'Did you say Francis Mason?'

'Yes.' Francis spoke a little thickly, for he wished to convey two things: first that he was apprehensive and secondly that he had been taking Dutch courage for his apprehensions. 'Yes,' he said again. He uttered a vague laugh, rather pleased with it. 'And I think I've done you.'

'I'm afraid I don't follow.'

'Come off it. You know what happened on Friday night; you know I was there.'

There was a pause before Amadeus said cautiously: 'Well?'

'Naturally boy-friend told me what it was all about.'

'Yes?'

'It was all about some money of mine. And I've still got it.' Francis Mason giggled tipsily. 'I'm not going to buy you off. I've beaten you – I'm quite smart, really. Those bonds are on their way to Candoro again. I don't mind telling you. There are some things you can't touch, Mister blasted Amadeus. The Bag ...'

'The Bag,' Amadeus said slowly.

'You heard me. It's Sunday today but the stuff'll be away tomorrow. Just to rub it in I don't mind telling you which of the boiled shirts holds it. It's a man called Gibb. There's nothing you

149

can do.' Francis breathed heavily into the receiver. 'I've bust you,' he said brutally. 'There's nothing you can do.'

'No,' Amadeus agreed, 'there's nothing I can do. But thanks all the same.'

He broke the connexion, dialling another number, and in twenty minutes the beautiful young man was with him. Amadeus spoke smoothly and with decision; he was Peter Amadeus again. The young man listened intently, nodding an occasional assent. 'It should work,' he said.

'You can see it's got to.'

'Yes, I can see that.'

'We shall need that taxi, of course.'

'We shall.'

'And afterwards . . .'

'And afterwards,' the young man said, 'afterwards Lucca and Levy.'

'You think they're up to it?'

'I think they're down to it.'

Amadeus said thoughtfully: 'We can't afford another failure.'

The young man smiled faintly. 'I'd gathered that.'

'Lucca and Levy are hardly intelligent.'

'They're not paid to be intelligent; they're bullies, hoodlums. But at that they're good.'

'I'd rather you were present.'

'I should simply be sick,' the young man said.

Peter Amadeus shrugged, but the young man didn't seem to resent it. He said quietly: 'The animals! They'll love it. God, how they'll love it!'

CHAPTER SIXTEEN

KENNETH GIBB found the parcel on his doormat when he returned to his flat at five o'clock. He had seen nothing like it, for, though modest in width and depth, it was not far short of two feet long. He broke the seals with curiosity, staring in amazement at the contents. He did not know the details, but he saw at once that these were Securities. The mental capital letter was his own. Like all officials ignorant of the affairs of lesser men he owned, but never admitted, a certain contempt for them. The contempt concealed an unnamed fear. Securities were the business of bankers and brokers, of men who made their livings in a gross, a daily competition. Moreover, in a sense it was a naughty word: there were rules about Securities, regulations about what the government servant might and might not buy. All this was instinctive, the conditioning of the official mind. One thing was certain, though: no official was blameless who retained on his premises bonds from an unknown source.... If it was unknown, Gibb thought unhappily. Francis Mason had assets in England, and as likely as not they were securities. Lately there had been a good deal of talk about them – tiresome, very unprofessional talk. Then he dumps the stuff on Kenneth Gibb, heaven knew why....

Kenneth Gibb saw it quite suddenly: it was a plant, a frame-up. Francis Mason had discovered his horns; he was framing his betrayer. Even now he might be talking to some senior, even on a Sunday, telling some story of blackmail, anything but the truth. Kenneth Gibb shuddered. If the bonds were discovered in his flat he hadn't a hope. He could tell them the truth, but deep in the truth was Francis's motive. The story was nonsense otherwise. He might be believed about the bonds, but even if he were, the smear ...

They'd probably hush it up – God knew they'd plenty of practice – but in the Service he'd be finished.

Kenneth Gibb made up his mind at once: he'd have to get in first. Get the bonds into the Office. Put them in the safe and take a proper receipt for them. Arrange to see Lampe-Lister first thing on Monday. Tell him the truth about the bonds and a lie about Mason. ... There had been some foolish quarrel, some insult imagined. You could think out the details tonight. But first get these damnable, these damning bonds away. Then you had a chance to be believed. But let them find you holding them, corroboration of Mason's complaint of blackmail. ...

Gibb shuddered again.

He put the securities into two briefcases and telephoned for a taxi. He didn't notice that another followed him.

At the Foreign Office he found the resident clerk, and together they sealed four envelopes. The resident clerk gave Gibb a safe receipt for four packages, contents unspecified.

Gibb began to breathe again.

He walked to Lampe-Lister's room, leaving an Immediate note for him in his secretary's office. As Gibb had expected Lampe-Lister's room was empty but, for a Sunday, there seemed to be an unusual activity. There were lights on the Important Floor, voices, the smell of urgency. From a window Gibb saw an official car drive into the courtyard fast. One of the ministers of state – Mr Tester, he noticed – got out of it. Mr Tester wasn't a man unconscious that he was a minister, but he went into the building at a smartish trot. Gibb smiled sourly: it was a flap again. He shrugged. Well, it couldn't be anything to do with Candoro: they'd have sent for him if it had been anything to do with Candoro.

In the courtyard Kenneth Gibb saw a taxi. He hesitated for lately he had been spending a good deal of money on taxis – more than he could afford. But in the end he hailed it. He had thinking to do; he had to consider the story he would tell Lampe-Lister in the morning. The taxi slid invitingly alongside and Gibb opened the door. He gave the driver his address.

He wasn't surprised when in Whitehall the taxi turned right-handed: on a Sunday, in clear traffic, that was probably the quickest way to Campden Hill. But in Parliament Square the driver swung unexpectedly left, accelerating down Bridge Street. Almost before Gibb realized it they were on Westminster Bridge. And still accelerating. Kenneth Gibb was annoyed. Who did the fellow think he was? Some out-of-town nobody who didn't know that Campden Hill was north of the river? The man would cut across the Albert Bridge again, through Chelsea, on to his proper route. But there would be another five bob on the clock. Gibb was furious. He rapped on the glass partition but the driver did not answer; he reached for the sliding panel, tugging at it.

It seemed to have jammed.

Kenneth Gibb sat back in a mounting anger. In Campden Hill, when they reached it, there would be the inevitable scene. He hated scenes and feared them: his instincts, his training were against them. Policemen weren't so ubiquitous on Campden Hill, and on a Sunday rarer than ever.

He looked from the window. They were across the bridge by now, but they hadn't, as he had hoped, turned right again. They weren't in the Lambeth Palace Road but going straight on. And faster – faster.

Kenneth Gibb recognized the Elephant. The driver passed it to his right, speeding again.

Gibb's anger began to fade before an emotion less agreeable. He rapped on the glass again. ... No answer. The driver was crazy. ... Then try the window. Gibb did so. It wouldn't move. So try the door. Not that at this speed you could jump for it.

Gibb tried the door. The handle moved freely but nothing else. He pushed furiously, sweating.

Nothing happened.

Kenneth Gibb sat back again, muttering, terrified. He looked from the window but he was wholly lost. Mean streets slid by, the ill-lit signs illegible, and presently the taxi slowed. At a corner a man appeared from nowhere; he spoke to the driver and the driver leaned forward below his steering wheel. There was a very faint click and the door of the taxi opened. The man got in. He shut the door and there was another click. The man was masked. He put an automatic in Gibb's ribs. The driver moved again. There was the hiss of escaping air, and the blinds of the taxi came smoothly down.

The little room was bare except for a wooden chair, shadowless in the light of a single naked bulb. Two men, hooded, waited in it silently. The man from the taxi pushed Kenneth Gibb to the chair and the waiting men tied him to it professionally. The man from the taxi said something to the others and they nodded. He glanced at Gibb; shrugged; left the room.

The taller of the hooded men said deliberately: 'Where are they?' His accent wasn't English.

'I don't know what you mean.'

'Don't stall. We know it all. Where are those bonds? Where are you keeping them? They're not in your flat.'

'I haven't got them. I ...'

The hooded man lit a cigarette. He smoked for a puff or two, then inspected his ash. He blew it away very carefully. The end of the cigarette glowed redly. Then, holding it, he walked to Kenneth Gibb. The lighted end he put between Gibb's lips.

Kenneth Gibb screamed.

'Nobody can hear you. Now ... Those bonds ...'

'I haven't got them. They're in the safe.'

'What safe?'

'The Office safe.'

'What office safe?'

'The Foreign Office.'

'You expect me to believe that?'

'It's the truth. I swear it. ...'

The hooded man blew on a second cigarette. 'No.' Gibb said. 'No. Please ...'

When he came to he was wet to the skin. The other man was standing over him, holding an empty bucket. The two were talking in a language which he understood, and what he heard froze him. He listened to himself say desperately: 'It's the truth, I tell you. I swear, I promise: ...'

'Shut up.'

The two men spoke again, in undertones now. The shorter shrugged. In English he said: 'We'd better make sure. It's worth another try.' He moved to Kenneth Gibb, untying an arm, taking the hand, looking at it curiously. 'Nice nails you've got.' He stood beside the chair and a little behind it, locking the free arm in simple judo. He didn't break the elbow but Gibb knew that he could. Gibb saw that the other had a knife. He struggled as he felt his hand taken – uselessly. On his elbow the pressure trebled suddenly. He screamed again.

... He was soaking a second time, shivering, shattered. Through the crimson mists of pain he saw his hand. He didn't believe what he saw. The men were talking again, softly, but Kenneth Gibb, his senses unnaturally sharp, could hear them.

'It might be the truth.'

'And again it might not.'

'You think he's holding out?'

'No. .... No. .... Not many hold against that. I don't think he's the type.'

'Then what?'

'Then he's useless.'

The taller man's shoulders rose and fell and the other nodded. He went behind Gibb's chair, feeling in his pocket. The blackjack was rubber, brief and dark. The shorter man looked at it reflectively, showing what he held to his companion. The taller nodded in turn.

The shorter put his left hand in what remained of Gibb's hair, forcing the head forward, tensing the neck. He raised his right.

Kenneth Gibb groaned once.

It was half past four when a frightened milkman discovered him. He found a policeman and the policeman an ambulance.

Sir Godfrey Henn sat in a room at the Foreign Office, very quiet and very alert. Mr William Lampe-Lister was with him, but the others had gone. The meeting – the important part of it – was over: the decisions had been taken. Gog and Magog lingered on.

Gog said reflectively: 'Lucky he understood their language. Lucky he lived a little.'

'Yes.'

'They were fools to talk so openly, but they were very low-level. I suppose they thought they were safe enough. That was luck for the Security Executive: Gibb heard enough to lead it to the men who count. This Amadeus, for one – it's been after him for years – and perhaps even to what's behind him. The small fry don't matter. Yes, it was lucky he lived a little.'

'And', Magog said slowly, 'lucky he finally died. Think of our position if he hadn't.' His voice changed to quotation. '"Foreign Office official, hideously mauled, found in a gutter in south-east London. Dies in hospital later." That's a scandal, but we can live with it. Just. We've had worse to live with lately. All those longhairs advising us about recruitment. . . . I can remember when there was a preliminary interview. No appeal. Then the final interview was worth 300 marks out of a total of 2,000. Since the top dozen candidates were all in a bracket around 1,400 the interview decided it. . . . Beautiful.' Lampe-Lister grimaced.

'Nowadays we listen to psychiatrists. We're madly democratic, and our reputation's never been lower. Yes, we're in for another scandal, and there's at least one paper which will splash it. Personally I don't blame them. But it's an ordinary sort of scandal, if you follow me – nothing political. Gib will have been doing something in south-east London – probably something distressing. Knowing our current aura everybody will assume it, and again I can't blame them. And in that particular world it isn't difficult to get into serious trouble. So it's just an ordinary, dirty Foreign Office scandal again. As we're running, that's almost old hat. I know who'll give it space, of course, and plenty.'

'So do I.'

'But many won't go after it, or not too seriously.'

'We can hope so,' Gog said.

'And if they do, they'll be fortunate to find the link. Gibb's dead – multiple injuries to the upper spine. The Executive knows the whole story, and a doctor who's been suitably impressed with the importance of leaving matters of state to statesmen.' Magog smiled ironically. 'Naturally that means you and me. And the Security Executive. I thought they took it very calmly, by the way. That man at the meeting – rather impressive, really.'

'Yes,' Gog said, 'very impressive indeed.'

Magog rose and Sir Godfrey lit a cigarette from his inevitable tattered packet. He was thinking that the man from the Executive had indeed been impressive. He had been the most senior of all Security men; he had already known the facts, and he had listened to the Foreign Office chewing them with a tolerant but polite detachment. To direct questions he had answered Yes or No: otherwise he hadn't spoken. Nobody, not even the minister, had cared to ask his plans.

Sir Godfrey Henn began to wonder what he would be doing if he were head of the Security Executive. This was a crisis – people you had been after for years. Now at last you had them; now you might make it stick. The Executive would be a hive of bees.

Or would it? he reflected. The Executive's head hadn't given the impression of a hive of bees. He had been greyly imperturbable, almost uninterested. Now you might make it stick, Gog thought again. But in England there were courts, notoriously prickly courts. There would be evidence to disclose, much of it matter which you would probably prefer not to. You knew it all now, but you might not be able to prove. Or it might pay you not to. Security was a delicate complex: blow one thing, get your squalid conviction, and you could easily compromise something else more important. And even if you hanged this Amadeus they could always find another.

Gog discovered that he was sitting bold upright. They ...? *They* were extremely formidable. Mr Peter Amadeus had put them at risk; he had let them down. They wouldn't be pleased with Peter Amadeus. It wasn't as though he were their only creature: there were bound to be others. No, they wouldn't be pleased with Peter Amadeus.

Gog shivered lightly. He was very glad he wasn't Mr Peter Amadeus.

An image floated across his mind, and he began to smile, for it amused him. ... The Head of Security was sitting in his office, his feet on the desk. Gog looked at his watch. The Head of Security would be drinking a glass of sherry. He was an authority on sherry. He would be doing precisely nothing, or not for forty-eight hours. Then he might not need to. Mr Peter Amadeus, stiff, wouldn't bother the Security Executive. The police could go after that one, and joy to them of it.

Gog walked slowly to his lunch. In the corner of the bar the Head of the Security Executive was drinking a glass of sherry. He gave to Sir Godfrey Henn a polite brief nod. But he did not speak to him. They had only been introduced that morning.

At London Airport Francis caught Menderez with ten minutes to spare. The Candoran Embassy hadn't been helpful: evidently it was in something like chaos. But he had spoken to Clare Kendrick, and not at the embassy, and from what she had told him he had made his guess.

Rightly, he thought now, as he walked quickly towards Menderez. Menderez was smiling but Francis was not. Francis said shortly: 'Don't be a fool.'

'Perhaps I was born one.'

'They'll get you the minute you land.'

'Not quite the minute I land. I won't go direct, you see. I'm going to B.A. I'll slip across the frontier when the dust settles.'

'But what do you think you can do?'

Menderez shrugged.

'You're crazy.'

Menderez said slowly: 'I'm going home. I must. It's different for you.'

'But why?'

'Putting it at the lowest, you have money.'

'Yes,' Francis said, 'I got it back.'

'Got it back?'

'I'll tell you sometime – now if you'll be sensible. Come and stay with us.'

'With *us*?'

'Yes. Clare and me.'

Menderez held his hand out. 'I'm delighted,' he said. 'Delighted.' He sounded it.

'Then come and keep us company.'

Menderez chuckled. 'On your honeymoon?'

Francis Mason stared levelly at Menderez, weighing a decision. 'You wouldn't be a stranger. I owe you an obligation . . . one of family.'

'You knew, then?'

'Yes.'

'Since when?'

'I've known for years.'

'And you really don't mind?'

'Why the devil should I mind? Good blood both sides. . . .'

Menderez said reflectively: 'You knew and you never used it. You could have, you know. When I was trying to squeeze you . . .'

Francis had dropped his eyes. 'I think you knew something too, something about Lavinia. You didn't use *that*, or never against myself.'

Menderez began to laugh. 'We're not very competent,' he said. 'Not at this sort of thing. We have inhibitions, and that's fatal. Not that I regret my scruples.' He held out his hand again. 'Be good to her.'

'I'll try.'

'Where are you going to live?'

'Not England.'

'Somewhere where there's sun?'

'Somewhere you can see it. We'll look around.' Francis Mason's manner changed to a sudden urgency. 'Come with us,' he said again. 'Don't throw it away.'

'Throw what away?'

'Your life. Everything.'

'Everything isn't so much. Not to me.'

Francis looked once more at Menderez. Menderez was smiling still, quite undramatic. But he was wholly serious; he had spoken of scruple and Francis understood him. There was a much grander word.

Francis said simply: 'May I say that I admire you?'

Menderez bowed.

The voice of a raucous ghost blared from the loudspeakers. It was croaking something about Channel Seven. . . . Seven, Francis thought for an instant. But he was without regret. He took Menderez's hand. '*Hasta la vista.*'

'*Adios.*'

'No,' Francis said, 'I'll see you again.'

For a second he was sure of it.